SHADOWS SLOW DANCING IN DERELICT ROOMS

BY

STEPHEN J. GOLDS

Outcast Press
Fiction From the Fringes

"But remember, my reader,

whom I hope to have travel far with me

through time and space.

Remember, please, my reader, that I

have thought much on these matters,

that through bloody nights and

sweats of dark that lasted years long,

I have been alone with my many selves

to consult and contemplate my many

selves."

~ Jack London, *The Star Rover*

ACKNOWLEDGEMENTS

Acknowledgments are really tough to write because I'm always worried about leaving people out. But, hell, here goes:

Megumi, thank you for taking in this flea-bitten mutt and thank you for being patient every time it tried to take a shite on the rug or chewed the furniture.

My daughters, M and N, Papa loves you more than you'll ever know.

My parents, family, and friends.

Thank you to Outcast Press for giving my words a home when no one else wanted to take the chance on them because they thought the content was too dark or the title of the novel was too long for marketing.

Thanks to all the writers and friends who have inspired me and continued to support me. You know who you are, right?

RIP Sarah Kane, who inspired me to write this novel and continues to inspire me daily.

Some fires burn too brightly.

This is an

absolute work of fiction

dedicated to

absolutely nobody.

ZERO

I was eight years old the first time I tried to hang myself.

Disorientated and manic at the time. My head felt as though it were a bright red helium balloon—pulsing, expanding. Full of blood. An inflating, gnawing black noise about to BURST!

The toys I had broken wouldn't fit back inside the toy box in my bedroom. The lid wouldn't close. It sat agape, staring at me—a toothless, grinning mouth. A monster I'd seen in a black-and-white movie once.

I remember I took a belt. Made of bright beads. North American Indian. A souvenir. Bought from a roadside stand by my father when he was in Canada with the military.

I wrapped it around my throat.

The small fingers on my hands worked the buckle fluently. Not impulsively. Instinctively. The finger-painted feeling in my guts, of fate.

I pulled the belt taut. Attaching the end to a small, plastic hook on the side of my cabin bed.

Leaned forward. Dangled there, weak at the knees. Choking myself.

There was nothing meaningful in it. Nothing heartbreakingly poetic. Just a brittle frustration—my broken toys wouldn't go where they were supposed to. I had to stand there, looking at them scattered across the floor. The shitty things I'd done. The good things I'd destroyed. Things broken. Things unfixable. Shapes and images out of order. Symmetry misaligned. Disarrayed like the things inside my head, in the space behind my eyelids. Black crayon scribbled on white scraps of paper crumpled up inside my brain.

The hook snapped.

I fell to the floor, gasping for air.

Technicolor reruns played in my brain—a couple of months prior, when I'd poured a can of paint thinner into the goldfish pond in my grandfather's back garden because I didn't like the jerky, non-symmetrical shapes the fish made in the pale green water. Their stupid, empty eyes disturbed me. I told my mother afterwards that the voices in my head had made me do it.

Coughing. Wheezing. Sniveling. Chewed fingernails clawed at the cheap, stained carpeting in my bedroom.

After a while, I crawled out of the room and went downstairs to eat a ketchup sandwich and watch cartoons on the television. The animated version of *Tales from the Crypt*. All while the belt hung loosely from my throat.

On my 28th birthday, I tried to hang myself again. I did it for the same reasons.

Catholics believe the souls of those who kill themselves haunt Purgatory. I guess that makes sense, doesn't it? If the jagged mess scratching around the insides of your skull and guts are Hell, when you die, you can't go where you've already lived.

For the purpose of clarity here, let me say, I am not a good person. I'm guilty of many sins. Venial and mortal. There isn't a place named Heaven for people like me.

I have maimed myself and wounded the ones I love. I have committed murder. And for selfish reasons.

I had only *tried* to murder myself. I had failed at that the same way I failed at everything else I ever attempted in my life.

I stay in Purgatory now. The shapeless mass between all things and not. A place by any other name is still the same.

Purgation.

Penance.

Mental Health Care Facility.

Limbo.

My Limbo has bright orange hallways and pale green walls. Soft, worn linoleum floors, pockmarked and cigarette burnt.

My Limbo stinks of stale sweat, chlorine, overflowing ashtrays, ancient piss, and cheap air freshener.

The soundtrack to my Limbo is hotel lobby Musak and the sighing, incessant chatter of lost souls. Scattered, misplaced minds.

My Limbo is watching shadowed reflections drift by in dirty, chicken-wire glass windows because the television in the common room is on the fritz. Not a place you stroll in sunshine. You live here slumped, loitering in a psychological damp. It's a jail cell for those already imprisoned within their own minds. Within the cages of their own hearts.

My Limbo is a red-bricked, under-funded mental health unit in North London.

My Limbo is where people go to get better, I am consistently told. I think it's simply a rest stop for suicides circling the runway and then crashing in empty cornfields. It's a perpetual lockdown in pharmaceutical bondage. Exhaling dust. Inhaling chemicals. Pupils dilated black holes.

My wounds are tentatively prodded at here. My traumas probed and examined—deliberated over. Evaluated and reevaluated. Notes are made.

Limbo is delusional. Limbo is psychosis. Limbo is my memory.

Limbo is where my love goes.

Limbo is where all love goes, finally.

Limbo is where I live with the shadow of a dead woman I'm still in love with. Her name is Amelie.

Limbo is where Amelie and I injure each other over and over whilst slow dancing to a record skipping on a turntable. Where we watch each other bleed out slowly whilst murmuring the words "I love you."

Limbo is where our pulsing hearts beat to a period mark. FULL STOP.

Limbo is where *they* finally assassinate Amelie and *they* put me out of my misery.

Limbo is where we stay together to really die together.

Limbo is The End.

Limbo is a circle.

Limbo is The Beginning.

ONE

A terminal sun beats down on us both, a tint of house arson orange. Standing waist-deep in an ocean aflame. Amelie's dark eyes flicker over me. Intense. Infinite. Eyes like November bonfires blazing. I'm the effigy. Her wicker man. A Guy Fawkes Night mannequin. She burns me up with a gaze soaked in gasoline anticipation, as though we're on the precipice of fucking or fighting. Her bleach blonde hair is tied up in a loose bun atop her head. She doesn't want to get it wet.

She's waiting for me. Or I'm waiting for her. I forget sometimes.

Moving her arms slowly, treading water. Skin porcelain-colored, ghostlike gliding through these glassy waters. Droplets caught on her cheeks as though she's been weeping. Maybe she has, but I don't want to think about that.

I don't know how long we've been looking at each other like this. Can't remember how we came to be here either. Treading water together. Here in the North Atlantic Ocean. The surf coming softly, rocking us back and forth like it's the death throes of a summer breeze. The tide sounds like the blood rushing through my twisted arteries.

Now I remember.

This is my Limbo, and we are weightless here. Timeless. Immortally mortal.

Three years. We were together three years before. Here. Amelie is dead now.

My love is dead.

I'm still dying.

And then she laughs. A serotonin-endorphin sound that always squeezes my heart in small fists. Snatching at my breath like fingertips running down starched, white bed linen. She isn't dead anymore. She's alive again.

I must remain still. Breathing shallow. The slightest movement could break my concentration. This moment. Shattering this intricate reflection that I painstakingly repainted within my mind.

I want her to stay. I want to stay. Here. Waist-deep in the ocean. With Amelie. Infinitely. Being with her again is all I needed. All I wanted.

Her lips are rose petals blossoming in speech now, her voice strange. The American accent gone. Words croak. Broken in shards. As though she has a sore throat. A bad cold. Not her own voice at all, but one thrown from the vocal cords of a ventriloquist sipping a glass of water on a bare, spot-lit stage. A slumped, hollow puppet grasped in a skeletal lap. Manipulated into reanimation. Amelie tells me she loves me. She forgives me. My mouth moves in sync with hers.

I know I'm only talking to myself, but at the same time I'm not.

She cups water in her palms and splashes me.

I remember this part well.

The time at the beach. One of our good days. The better days. Standing in the ocean together like that, like this, we could almost forget the crimes we'd committed against each other.

Stupid. We thought the ocean could wash us clean, but there was a death between us. Death is an oily, dark mass that only grows and deepens. Staining all it touches.

Darkness eats everything—absolutely.

I hold her close, tightly wrapping my arms around her, pulling her hips into me—the same way I did back then. When it was real. Really happening and not just a memory.

Amelie's bikini top is black. I blink and it's red, then white. I blink again and it's back to black. Small details change here. Amelie never changes. She is the one consistency. Her breasts full, heavy against my chest. She has no heartbeat because she is dead. I imagine I can feel it beating through her bikini top, drumming into my skin, into my blood like the needle of a tattooist.

Lifting herself out of the water, she pulls herself up my shoulders, ties her thighs and legs around my waist.

She was always the noose I wanted to hang myself in— I mentioned that to my therapist once. She frowned and scribbled it down in her notes. I guess it was important to her somehow. She doesn't know.

Amelie is dead. She left me dying.

I am the ghost now.

I have brought us back together through time and space.

I run my lips along the nape of her neck. The scent of her perfume, Chanel No. 5—a Christmas gift she drunkenly threw at me and smashed against her bedroom wall one night— mixing with the seawater and sunscreen filling my lungs. Amelie is smoke inhaled into the very fabric of what I am. Of what little remains of me now, she is gone.

Her mouth on mine. Lips tasting of ocean spray and cherry red lipstick.

I wish I was dead like her, and this moment was my afterlife. Lived on repeat. Over and over again.

Children were wading in rock pools on the shore that day, searching for crabs, shells, or coral. Amelie watched them for a long moment and then turned to look at me. Then we both stared into the horizon for a long time, not saying anything.

There was a pure white lighthouse stabbing the sky on the cliffs in the distance. The cliffs—shards of glass fallen from a picture frame. Broken, beautiful things. Amelie in my arms. A broken beautiful thing. It was those cliffs that she would take her life leaping from. Glaring down on us. Knowing the soul that I sold for a thousand pounds and a momentary feeling of selfish relief. Murder. Knowing. It was my fault. I pushed her from those cliffs. Killed her. I murder everything I love. I'm the serial killer of my own transient moments of happiness.

I'm trembling now. I don't know why. It's not cold. The water feels like summer rain. We're in Margate, New Jersey. At a beach five minutes' walk from Amelie's mother's house. We'd flown out from Heathrow for a short break. Amelie called it "our American getaway." We're staying at a storm-damaged motel by the shore. A room with a sea view, peeling paint, and a clogged toilet. Fucking, eating, drinking, sleeping. When the sun sets, it colors the small room a deep orange. It's as though we drown in flames as we lie there on the bed, looking into each other's faces.

We hit the casinos in Atlantic City for the first couple of days and then Amelie takes me to meet the mother she hates. Her father left the family when she was a child and then drank himself to death. Her mother is a somber woman, walking around the cluttered house in a constant state of shock and confusion. Her slow movements are like ash-colored evening shadows cast along a cracked wall. We leave soon after arriving. I don't know why Amelie hates her mother. She never tells me.

Amelie hated many people. *This person abused her. This one was poison. This one spread lies. This one abandoned her.* They'd all done her wrong somehow, somewhere, and she painted them all black. She painted me black too, but she always came back. Until she didn't. She said I was the only person who could save her. I couldn't save her from myself though.

I never met her friends. I don't think she had any. Beautiful women like Amelie never really do. Everyone tries to own beauty and if they can't, they resent it. Tarnish it or destroy it. Beautiful women like Amelie are suns locking all the other stars and planets at distance to orbit. She had many orbiters. Always someone waiting in her waiting room.

Amelie and I—loners who couldn't stand to be alone with ourselves.

She takes my hands in hers, pulling me deeper into darker currents.

I follow her into that darkness. The water icy now. Freezing. Amelie doesn't seem to notice. She is smiling at me.

I lose grip of her hand for a split second. Her face changes. Fades. Ripples. Shimmers. Blurs.

Concentrate. Remember.

Holding her in my arms. The way her body moves against mine. Her mouth on mine. The sand clinging to our skin. Her long hair twisting through my fingers.

I remember.

We fuck slowly on an isolated part of the beach, hidden by dunes and the night. It's beautiful because it feels as though it will be our last time. Every time we fuck feels like our last time. A sexual eulogy. A funeral march into the depths of each other. Ashes to ashes. Dust to dust.

After, her head resting on my chest, I open my eyes and look at the midnight sky. Think I can see the Milky Way. Thousands of bright, shattered, blinking things. Stolen diamonds on a black silk sheet.

Those stars are gone now. Only a decomposing memory of that sky remains.

I don't want to look up.

I'm staring down at the water cupped in my palms. There's only the pale reflection of my own face.

I'm not really here.

There's a heavy splash. Something vicious breaking into the surf. Primeval. Hospital ward pale green. Streetlight yellow-eyed. Twisting madly. A razor-tipped snout sneering above the surface of the water. The only animal I dream about. A large crocodile circles us. It submerges.

Amelie is gone.

I'm alone.

Is this real or a memory? A dream or déjà vu?

I don't know anymore.

I've lost myself again. Become confused.

Limbo is a circle.

I open my mouth and the ghost of myself seeps out like a held breath.

Waves slap me hard across the face, stinging my eyes. They burn, tear up. Amelie is cursing at me now. Screaming at me from the shore. Calling me a piece of shit.

The razor-tipped jaws of the crocodile clamp down on my flesh, tearing and ripping through me. I watch it tear me apart like I'm watching an animal documentary on a television set in a room far away.

The water is such a deep, bitter red, it's almost black.

I close my eyes and open them again.

I'm somewhere else. Somewhere new and old.

TWO

Morning now.

I'm sitting at a small table across from Amelie. In a coffee shop we happened upon while walking down the far end of the beach. Remember it well. Beach-bum inspired interior. A pale green surfboard above a varnished bamboo bar. The walls were painted a bright orange like the setting sun. We ate breakfast here every day while we were in Margate, New Jersey, attempting to mend the splintered bones of our relationship.

I look down at the plate in front of me. Half-eaten pancakes and blueberry French toast. I don't remember ordering food. I glance around for a waitress. The place is dead.

Amelie is dead.

I am dying.

My clothes soak through. Dripping puddles on the tile. Pooling on the tabletop.

I know it isn't seawater. It's rainwater. I am full of rainwater. Feel it pumping through my veins and arteries. Leaking from my pores. My heart is a sewer drain, clogged. Flooded. Stagnant.

I'm standing in the rain on a street in London for a split second and then I'm back sitting in the coffee shop.

Amelie sits with her legs crossed high, denim skirt hitched up, showing off her thighs. Sipping black, decaffeinated coffee from a white mug. The mug says **happy dayz** in a childish blue script. There's a crack at the lip of it. She's spreading instant Kodak photographs she's taken of us across the tabletop. Fanning them out in order like puzzle pieces of what we are when we're together like this. What we were.

"Amelie, I know this is just a memory, but it feels like déjà vu. Down here. In my stomach," I say, grasping at my belly like I've been sucker punched in the guts.

"That's probably what a baby feels like when it moves. When it kicks. But what would I know about *that*, right, Vincent?" Amelie whispers, staring into the space above my right shoulder.

I turn to see who she's looking at. There's no one there.

She flicks the long, blonde hair back over her right shoulder, pouting at me the way she always did when pissed off. Her mobile phone is face-down in front of her. It's vibrating. Over and over again. The noise of it like the ultrasound of the child we aborted before we traveled to her hometown to run from what we had done. What I had done.

"Who's calling you, Amelie?" I stutter. Breathless. Choking. There's a belt around my throat. Made of bright beads. North American Indian. A souvenir. Bought from a roadside stand by my father when he was in Canada with the military. I untangle it from around my throat and let it fall to the damp floor. I blink and it's gone.

"I don't know. Probably my mom," Amelie sighs too deeply, picking up the phone and sliding it into her designer leather purse. Out of sight. Out of reach. Still vibrating madly. Her eyes don't meet mine.

I am cut-throat and tongue-tied. I chew at a hangnail. Tasting a bitter, electric sting of blood. The blood is the only thing that's real here. "Really? They're blowing up your phone like crazy. Why don't you just answer it? It might be important, don't you think? An emergency. Something like that?"

"What's on my phone will only hurt us both, so what's the point in remembering all that negative shit again, Vincent? Why?" She frowns down into the coffee mug. Shrugs like she doesn't give a shit.

"This isn't how it happened at all," I say.

"What do you mean?" she asks.

"In the coffee shop. In your hometown. It wasn't like this. This is wrong."

"It's your movie, isn't it, Vincent? Why have the phone here at all if it upsets you?"

"My clothes are soaking wet," I say, showing her the water dripping from my body.

"I'm completely dry." She picks flint from her skirt, rolling it between her fingers.

"Why? Can you just tell me why?" I don't know why I ask. My lips flap open like a flesh wound and the question crawls out with a bitter whiskey aftertaste—even though I can't remember the last time I drank. Alcohol has a bad effect on me. Makes me do painful things. Words clatter to the tabletop with the teeth falling loose from my mouth. A canine, a molar. I pick them up, cringingly examine them and drop them clattering into a glass ashtray.

"You came here in the storm, remember? It was fucking Hollywood-esque." She shrugs her bare shoulders. The thin strap to her bikini top falls down her arm.

I want her so much. Somewhere, I'm on my knees on a London street in the rain. But that's a different place. Somewhere I don't want to go to again. The day Amelie killed herself. "I just want to be with you. I wanted to say I'm sorry for what I did." My voice breaks and I feel like I'm reading from a script. The words have already been uttered—only in a different location. A different time. Echoes from other realities. What-might've-beens. What-could've-beens. What has been. Memories. There are multiple universes where we exist, and Amelie is dead in every single one. I'm dying everywhere I might have existed.

"Why?" Her eyes don't shimmer now. They burn. She is liquid fire.

Somewhere, a door slams shut. My hands are trembling. "For what I made you do. I want you to forgive me," I say.

"I… love you…Vincent. There's nothing left to forgive. It's over."

The phone rings out again. Another door slams.

"Can't you stop those people from interrupting for five fucking minutes? I'm spilling my guts out over here, Amelie." I realize I'm shouting. Swallow. Breathe. More teeth rattle out onto the tablecloth. I quickly pick them up, self-conscious, and push them into the side pocket of the dirty bathrobe I suddenly realize I'm wearing. There's no belt on the bathrobe. No laces in the trainers on my feet either. For my own safety.

"I'm not really here, Vincent. These are your memories. Your little traumas, your regrets—not mine. You're working your way through it all, aren't you? Have you been taking your medication, Vincent?"

I'm confused. *Who's talking here?* My stomach hurts. This never goes the way I want it to.

I fork rain-soggy food into my mouth to dull the sharp, boiling pain in my intestines. It tastes of nothing. Empty, as though I'm chewing at mouthfuls of stale, recirculated air. Dust. Gnawing at my swollen tongue. "The meds give me cotton mouth. Make me confused," I say, picking up a glass container of maple syrup and trying to pour it onto the breakfast. Nothing comes out.

Amelie brushes a few loose strands of peroxide-blonde hair from her face and gazes at me seriously. Frowning again. Her eyes are black holes in the cosmos, sucking me in. She's the most beautiful woman I've ever known. She looks like Marilyn Monroe.

There is a razor-tipped flower inside my skull, blossoming. The petals draw blood. Another migraine. My tongue feels too large in my jaw.

"You want to fix things? You can't. Not here. They will always break us apart, you know that?" Her voice is strange again, sounding more like my own than hers.

"Who? Your mother? She seemed okay to me," I say, still snatching glimpses towards where the phone screams in her purse. One of the instant Kodak photographs is of Amelie falling from the cliffs underneath the white lighthouse. I turn it over, so I don't have to look at it.

She is already dead.

I am still dying.

"No, the people in this place." She glances back over her shoulder at a couple guys standing outside, loitering around the coffee shop carpark. Her fingers to her lips now. *Shhhh.*

The men are wearing blue doctors' scrubs. I can remember their names. The muscular skinhead is called Michael; I imagine he speaks with a thick South London accent. The skinnier guy is Greg; he plays bass guitar in some shitty garage band. They're both fucking pricks. I don't blame them. They shouldn't be here though. They never should've been.

"The people here. With you," she says again.

"Yeah, them. I don't remember them being here before," I say. "They weren't in Margate. They came around later, didn't they? I'm confused again. Mixed up. I had to take my meds this morning."

Amelie stares through me.

The orderlies, Greg and Michael, blink out of existence.

I grind my teeth until my jaw aches and try to focus.

It's only Amelie and I in the coffee shop now. It's only us.

It's only us.

It's only us.

It's only us.

Mouth cotton-wool dry. Throat aching. The meds. The meds.

Have you been taking your meds, Vincent?

The air ripples as though a heat wave is passing through the place. Things lose color. Someone starts yelling somewhere. A woman cursing in a shrill wail. "Someone's trying to fucking poison me!" she screams. "Those fucking people are poisoning me."

Cracks split up the walls. Torn plaster dust falls from the ceiling like raindrops. Particles catch the yellow morning sun, coating Amelie's hair and face in a chalky powder. Snowflakes.

I remember the Christmas we spent in a small bed and breakfast by the railway station in Liverpool. On a street after midnight, slow dancing with Amelie underneath a streetlamp to a car radio. Snow on the wind like static on a broken television set. Making love on sheets that smelled of hotel shampoo as trains clattered by into the night.

That's a good memory, but I'm not there. *Why can't I relive that memory?*

The ground trembles. Cutlery and porcelain rattle and fall from tabletops. The pancakes on the shattered plate in front of me have grown pale green and moldy.

"You're losing me, Vincent. Everything is rotting here. Everything is dead. You're running out of time. Why can't you just accept that?" Amelie cringes. Frigid fingers find the side of my face.

"This is just temporary, Amelie," I stutter.

"Death is never temporary, Vincent. It's for good. But I'm not alone. Someone's here with me. You're alone," she whispers.

I reach across the table and take her other hand. Squeeze. Her skin feels rough like a starched hospital bedsheet.

Another aftershock rips through the coffee shop.

"It's just us again. Just us," I try to swallow. Can't. Cough. Blink.

A baby is crying from the room above us and won't stop. The shrill cries vibrate through the ceiling.

"That could've been our child, Vincent. Up there. He's in Heaven now. Do you know how much that hurts me? That's why I had to hurt you, too. I wanted to hurt you the way you hurt me."

I look around at my fading fantasy as it gets torn apart. "It's okay now. There's no one else here. It's just us. This is a place just for us, Amelie. I made it just for us."

For a micro-second, I'm in a small, stale room. Someone is yelling.

Focus. Concentrate.

The coffee shop.

The windows explode into diamonds, scattering like rainfall across the worn carpeting. Chairs topple over. The surfboard above the bar falls like a bomb and crumbles into sand. The baby's wailing reaches a fever pitch and cuts out as abruptly as it started.

"No, they're still here. Those people. They've always been here. They'll always be here. Watching us. Watching you. You're never going to leave this place, are you, Vincent? You're losing me and losing your mind and you're never getting better. You need to wake up now. Wake up and smell the fucking coffee! You need to leave here, Vincent." Amelie's lips are baby blue. Dead.

I try to remember the way they felt on my skin. What shapes they made when they spoke my name. When they really uttered the words, *I love you.* "I don't know what you mean. I really don't want to think about anyone else, Amelie. I want to concentrate on you. Just you. Concentrate. I need to concentrate."

"They're breaking us up. You're losing me again, Vincent. You'll lose me and maybe it's for the best. I'm fucking dead. It's over. Just go home, Vincent!"

"No, I don't want to lose you, Amelie. I need you. I'm *not* going to lose you again, I promise."

She laughs bitterly. "You never made a promise you could ever keep, Vincent. Not one single time."

"Amelie…" I trail off, the words slurring together. My head hurts badly.

"You really have to go," she says. She's holding the paper check in her fingers now. "It's like a thousand or something for the procedure. I'm not a British national, so none of that wonderful National Health Service for me. Besides," she says, tossing it onto the damp tabletop. Water soaks into the paper. "You broke it, you fucking bought it."

"What do you mean?"

"I mean, you were the one who wanted the fucking procedure; you can pay for the fucking thing."

"What procedure?"

She impatiently clicks her fingers in my face. "Concentrate, Vincent! Concentrate! The baby I wanted, and you didn't. The one you made me get rid of. Murder. You didn't even go to the clinic with me either, Vincent. Did you? You left me there by myself. I needed you to be there with me so badly. You'd said you'd be there. I tried my best to smile again and pretend like everything was okay after that. That I was okay. But I wasn't. I wasn't okay at all. They ripped me apart that day and where were you? You weren't anywhere. Drinking! Drunk! You have only yourself to blame for all this shit, Vincent. You're not a good person. You're a complete piece of shit. You're awful. We're both awful people. And awful people do awful things to each other, don't they?"

"Please don't talk like that, Amelie." Even here in a dream, the pleading tone of my voice causes my face to flush red. *Is this a dream?* It's not a memory anymore. Nor fantasy. It's the landscape of my guilt.

"I changed after that. It changed me a lot. We changed. Like broken glass. Just cutting each other every time we touched." She smashes the **happy dayz** coffee mug on the edge of the table, startling me, picks a piece of the white porcelain from the mess. She drags it jaggedly along her left wrist in quick, slashing motions. "See! Like this, Vincent. We were just. Like. Fucking. This!"

I watch her, unable to move. No blood pours from the wound. Red rose petals fall from the gashes, slowly floating down to the tabletop. They turn brown, then black, then into ash.

She tosses the shard of mug onto my plate, rests her chin on her hand. Elbow in the pile of ash and dust. "What's the matter, Vincent? Don't like the sight of a little blood?"

"You never did that. Cut yourself like that."

"Yeah, I did. You know I did. It was the only thing that ever made me feel at peace with myself. The only thing that made me feel anything. I told you that. I told you that many times."

"Not in Margate, you didn't, and not with that mug."

"Maybe you *are* getting confused, Vincent. Mixed up. That's the problem with lies, isn't it? They become all jumbled up in your head so you can't keep track of them. We both know all about that, don't we? Lies. Lies. Lies. Are you taking your meds, Vincent?"

"I'm trying not to. I already said, they make me confused. I can't concentrate at all."

She takes a long sip of coffee from the now reformed mug and grins at me. "Anyway, you have to go back, Vincent. Just go home. Go home before I call the cops!"

"No, there's still time. I'll pay," I say, trying to find my wallet for the bill. There are no pockets in my trousers because I'm not wearing any. I'm wearing the bathrobe. The bathrobe without a belt over shorts and a short-sleeved shirt. I haven't had a wallet in months. Haven't needed one.

When she passes over the worn, folded piece of paper, I open it up to see it isn't a bill for the abortion at all, but her suicide note. Her flowery cursive sloping across hazy blue lines.

"Here you go. That belongs to you now, Vincent. It will always belong to you," she murmurs. My lips move in sync with hers again.

"I can save you, Amelie. I'll go to the lighthouse and fix it. Stop you from dying. Fix everything. Keep you."

Amelie snorts in disbelief, wiping at a crimson teardrop that has leaked from her left eye and dribbles down her rotting skin. "You can't save me, Vincent. I'm not even dead. You are. You're the one who's dead, Vincent. Go home!"

I'm eight years old and choking, dangling from my cabin bed.

The first time I try to hang myself.

Playthings scatter across the worn carpet.

Broken, damaged things.

The bell above the coffee shop door rings out, startling me again.

The door is closed, but there is a heavily built woman standing in the entrance now. Half in, half out. A monster from a black-and-white movie I saw once. Her coloring is off. Too bright in places. Too dull in others.

I know her. Yes, of course I do.

She's a Canadian woman who lives in High Barnet, North London. Not far away at all. Her name is Katherine. She's one of the clinic's consultant psychiatrists. My therapist.

I turn back to Amelie. She's frozen, warped like a picture on a stalled computer screen. Her features blur.

"Vincent?" Katherine calls softly. "Vincent?" she taps on the wall with her knuckles, in the tune of "Shave and a Haircut." The walls of the coffee shop aren't orange anymore. They're a pale green and then they're a faded, grimy gray.

I try to ignore her.

She's a ghost. A daydream. A bad memory. A figment of my imagination.

She's not really here. I'm not here. I'm there, in the coffee shop with Amelie.

"Vincent!" she calls out again. A little louder. More authoritative.

The woolen sweater pulled tight over her plump body is a luminous red flag. The coffee shop fades and shrivels—a photograph left in the sun.

I place my hands to Amelie's cheeks. She crumbles. Beach sand piles up in my palms.

She's gone.

I'm dragged back to Purgatory.

THREE

On the beaches of Limbo. Washed ashore. A recovery unit my younger sister, older brother, and mother have all been patients in before me. One time or another. The place is almost like a family institution. A genealogy tree riddled with mental disease and madness—passed down generation to generation like blond hair and blue eyes.

There's nothing that aches more than getting ripped from the womb of a happy memory or dream of someone who loved you once but doesn't anymore. That is real love and the crippling wounds it leaves behind, but they'll never put that in a fucking Hallmark card.

The clinic. The ward. Bricks and mortar. These bitter Technicolor realities that belong to me like a name stitched into the lining of a jacket. Tattooed into flesh.

Welcome home, Vincent. You miserable piece of fucking shit.

My eyes take a moment to adjust to the light. Dry as beach sand. Amelie's last letter, her suicide note, still gripped in my fingertips.

I'm sitting on a bed. It's my bed. There's a simple desk, a plain chair, and a scarred chest of drawers. It's my room. Not the room I had when I first arrived. The room stinking of vomit, piss, and disinfectant. The room people call the *Observation Room.* Spoken of in funeral wake whispers.

I kept the door wide open for the first three days. There was a small window that could only be pushed open five centimeters wide. The staff checked on me constantly. Yanking the sheets from my face in the night while I slept, shining a flashlight in my eyes to make sure I wasn't dead. Observation. Standing outside the toilet cubicle whenever I had to piss or shit. Observation. I was pumped full of drugs and babied into a softly animated, shuffling slumber. Easier for the staff that way. They were overworked. Tired. Wanting an easier shift. An easier life. *Who doesn't?*

The first few days in observation, I couldn't tell what was sleep and what was consciousness. Still can't recollect most of what happened to me there. Then. It's for the best.

Now, I'm in what they call a *recovery* room. Mixed in with the other patients, completely. No longer deemed an immediate danger to myself. Whatever that means.

The staff still check on me constantly, but I can close the door when I want to and take a crap in semi-private peace. Even with the door closed, they knock every five minutes. Checking. Rechecking. Confirming. Reconfirming.

"Are you okay in there, Vincent?"

Okay.

What a strange word *okay* becomes when you hear it barked at you through different doorways in a mental facility after you've tried to kill yourself. I don't really know what okay means anymore. Not sure I ever did. *Does anyone?*

I always tell them, the orderlies, nurses, or whatever they're called, I'm changing my clothes. It's simpler that way. If they think it's strange that I spend hours changing my clothes, they don't say anything. Maybe they think I have severe OCD like one or two of the other patients. Maybe they think I'm masturbating, knocking one out, but I haven't done *that* in months. Haven't had the energy, nor the notion to.

"How are you feeling today, Vincent?" Katherine asks, putting a subtle twist to the question I'm sick to death of hearing, as she shuffles further into my room. Greg and Michael, the "support" staff, hover like blowflies behind her in the pale green hallway. They're "back up" in case I become *aggressive* again.

In the ward, being considered *aggressive* is speaking in a voice slightly louder than a murmur. When my mother mentioned on the medical forms that I'd boxed a little as an amateur, they almost didn't take me in at all. Said they didn't have the "facilities" for me. Wanted to put me up somewhere like the hospital from *One Flew Over the Cuckoo's Nest*. Properly section me. In a proper nut house. My broken, crumpled face should have reassured them I wasn't any good at the sport.

Katherine stares at me, waiting for me to answer her. I stare back. My eyes sting. The migraine has become a mushroom cloud of clotted blood in my brain. I blink first. Clear my throat and stumble over words. I'm pissed off at the disruption and still punch-drunk from the morning's meds I haven't had a chance to vomit up. They're in my bloodstream now. Floating through my crooked veins. The gray light of day drifting through the window is like cigarette smoke stabbing at my train of thought. Jarred. Disoriented. No wonder I can't concentrate, and my memories are mixed up and confused. That's the reason reliving my life with Amelie didn't work and was all fucked up. My subconscious wearing Amelie's skin and tormenting me.

I dry-cough. "Yeah, you disturbed me, Nurse Ratched," I finally mumble.

Katherine's rosy complexion flushes a deeper shade of crimson. She spits out something imitating a chuckle. I know she dislikes my nickname for her, almost as much as she probably dislikes me. She's paid to pretend though. Earns her money pretty well. "Oh, sorry, were you about to write a letter or something, Vincent?" She jabs a stubby finger towards the piece of paper in my fingers. Amelie's suicide note. The bitch knows full well what it is and is fucking with me.

"No," I say, folding it neatly in two and sliding it into the breast pocket of the stained shirt underneath my robe. Patting at the soft fabric. I clear my throat again and don't know why.

"We had a one-on-one meeting scheduled for this morning, Vincent. At 10:30. I thought we both agreed on the time. Why didn't you come this time? Did you forget again?" She talks faux-cheerful, grinning at me as though I'm a kid and she's a children's television presenter explaining how to make something out of papier-mâché. Her teeth are too white and too straight. I wonder if they're dentures and fold my arms across my chest, tight.

"One on one. Makes it sound kind of like a game. A fight or something I can win, doesn't it?"

She picks flint from her sleeve. Doesn't answer. Passive aggressively waiting for me.

"No, I didn't forget about the meeting. I just didn't feel like it today. I wanted to relax alone in my room and meditate. I have a headache. A migraine, actually," I say.

Katherine runs a small hand over the mousy hair pulled into a tight ponytail on her perfectly round head, glancing over at my bed. Eyeing the books, a postcard of a white lighthouse, and the Kodak photographs carefully spread across the sheets. "Meditating again, huh? Is that what you're doing?" She nods solemnly, as if conversing with herself. The way, I guess, all psychotherapists feel they're supposed to.

I nod too, pinching at my thick, greasy beard that seems to have sprouted overnight with my thumb and forefinger. I never tell them what I'm really doing in my room. Traveling back into my memories to relive the past. In a place where every word you utter is analyzed and drugs are prescribed for quick answers, it would be crazy to tell them anything at all.

"You didn't eat breakfast again today, too, I've been told. What's wrong, Vincent? You really don't like the food here?" she asks, shuffling a couple of steps closer.

"And *I* told *you* already, I'm fasting," I say, subconsciously rubbing a hand over my empty stomach and then quickly pulling it away.

"Yes, I *know* we discussed the fasting *already*. You told me you had to fast because of your faith. You said you were a Muslim convert. However, I spoke to your parents the last time they visited, Vincent, and they said *that* is not true at all. They said you were raised Catholic. Besides, it's not even the time for Ramadan. I Googled it." She gurgles that fake laughter again.

"Are you questioning my devotion to Buddha?" I ask.

"No, no, not at all. I'm just trying to help you, Vincent. That's all. And I believe it's Allah the Muslims worship, not Buddha."

"Yeah, I know, Nurse Ratched," I sigh. "It was an attempt at humor. Can't somebody try and make a joke around here without it being taken seriously and analyzed?"

Katherine blinks and stares. Her mouth a puckered naval.

"Never mind. Look, I don't feel like talking to anyone. Why can't people just leave me the hell alone for a little while?"

Katherine picks up a book from the bed and examines it. "*The Star Rover* by Jack London…Jack London, didn't he write the novel about the wolf or something?"

"Yeah, he did," I say. "*White Fang.*"

"Wasn't he an anti-Semite though?"

"What? How would I know?"

She belly-laughs.

I don't know why. I wonder if it's a comment about my Jewish surname or if she's testing to see if I'm an anti-Semite. I cringe, that's all the energy I have left to do.

"What's this one about then? Must be good, I always see you reading it," she says, flicking through the pages like an animated flipbook. The cool whisper of air from the paper fans my face. It smells like the secondhand bookstore I bought it from before everything went to shit. The scent of a life before. I want to cry. I feel like crying often but can't. The tears don't come. They just fester inside, boiling at the bottom of my intestines. Clogging me up and constipating me. Haven't cried since the night Amelie killed herself.

The book in Katherine's crab-like hand is my guidebook, my bible. It's about a man escaping his misery by traveling through time and space within his mind. It's supposed to be based on a true story, told to Jack London by an ex-convict who spent a lot of time locked-up in the hole. I live by the book now.

I swivel my eyes up to meet Katherine's. Neck stiff. Try to clear my throat again. Cough. Swallow back a bitterness tasting like the rusty wreckage of a train crash, with a slimy, pharmaceutical mucus.

"I don't know. I'm not a book critic. Why don't you just read it yourself?" I shrug lopsidedly, reaching out to take it back. A grin painfully carved into my face.

Katherine sidesteps my jab like a seasoned boxer, holding the novel slightly out of reach. I wonder if she's going to toss it to one of her little buddies, her flying monkeys, Greg and Michael, and I'll be forced to play Piggy in the Middle like some stupid fucking kid in primary school. "Can I borrow this one?"

I snatch the book out of her stubby fingers, push it under my arse, so I'm sitting on it.

She gasps and jumps back at the speed of my hand. A palm spread over her flat chest like a dead spider. Playing the shocked and appalled card.

"No, this is my copy. Mine. Sorry. You should go to the library. They'll probably have a couple of editions you can borrow."

"Okay, then. Maybe I'll do that. Haven't been to a library in a while though, not since my college days. I'll just pop into the bookstore, buy a copy in town on my way home."

I nod along with her as though I'm listening. *Yeah, yeah, yeah.* Trying to speed the interaction up so I can be alone again. So I can "meditate." So I can be with Amelie again. I need to go to the lighthouse and stop her from jumping. Stop her from killing herself. I can save her. Holding onto that is keeping me alive more than any of their drugs or therapy sessions ever could. I've been trying so damn hard. They say time travel is impossible, but it isn't if you have memories. An imagination. I can live in the past if I want to. Change the past if I want to. I saw on a documentary once about these Chinese monks who can meditate so deeply, it's like they're dead. Their heartbeats slow down to almost nothing. Like a physical hibernation. Some of them can stay like that for decades. Anything is possible.

A panpipe version of Elvis' "Can't Help Falling in Love" starts seeping out from tinny speakers in the hallway ceiling. I know the next song will be "Right Here Waiting." Then it'll be The Beach Boys' "God Only Knows," followed by Eric Carmen, Harry Nilsson, and then Chris Isaak. I'm not psychic. They play the same heartbreak Musak on repeat. Who knows why? Listening to the panpipe version of "All by Myself" while watching the other patients rock themselves back and forth, scratching at the scars of their self-harms...makes me want to try to hang myself all over again. Maybe that's what they want. I'm sure they're fucking with us.

I pick up the photographs of Amelie and me, carefully, in their special order and place the thin pile into the breast pocket of my shirt with Amelie's letter. Close to the slow drumming of my overmedicated heart.

Amelie, my heart will always be this suicide note you left behind.

Norman, the 45-year-old manic-depressive in the room next to mine, starts pounding on the wall. I wonder if he's banging his head again. Michael jogs past my doorway. His Adidas Superstars squeak over the linoleum like footsteps from gym class a lifetime ago. I hear mumbled voices. Norman shouts something and then the banging ceases. The abrupt, demented silence screams louder instead.

I nod towards Katherine. "You know, Norman next-door was banging his head against the wall for 45 minutes yesterday and none of you people did jack shit about it. I couldn't concentrate at all. And Mark, that nervous guy who has a bloody nose all the time, was locked outside in the courtyard. I can't remember what day it was, but he was. Locked out. In the rain, too, Nurse Ratched. What kind of a place are you people running here? I know the NHS is understaffed and underfunded, but what the actual fuck?"

"I can see you're concerned about the other patients' welfare and that's very kind and compassionate of you, Vincent. But please remember cursing and using foul language at staff is never tolerated. Consider that a warning."

"People are using bad language here all the time. We're sick. Sick people can't control what they say."

She puts her hands on her hips, shoves her chin up into the air. "It's not up for debate, Vincent. Now, as for what you've said about Norman and Mark, I promise I'll look into those matters, of course." She makes a soft clucking noise in her throat. I guess it's supposed to be soothing and sympathetic but sounds more like an impatient growl. She pushes her greasy spectacles up her nose with her middle finger. "However, much more importantly, I'd like to keep to our counseling schedule, Vincent. If that's quite all right with you? You're taking precious time away from the other patients. I want you to think about that the next time you don't feel like coming."

"I don't see how any of it's helping. All the talking. Blah. Blah. Blah. It's not helping me. All that self-pity and complaining. *'No one likes me. People are whispering about me. The world is against me. I was abandoned as a child. Everyone I love leaves me.'* Blah. Blah. Blah."

"Vincent, you're here by court order because you're very unwell. You tried to take your own life, amongst *other* things. How do you suppose you'll ever get better if you're not participating fully in the counseling sessions, not eating properly, not taking the medications prescribed? We are here to help you. We're not your enemies. I'm not Nurse Ratched and you're not Jack Nicholson."

"Hold on a minute, I *am* taking the pills. The venlafaxine, and the Seroquel for anxiety and insomnia. I don't even have any insomnia but I'm popping all the pills you people give me. I'm a walking pharmacy. Shuffling around like a zombie in *The Walking Dead.*"

Michael's face reappears in the doorway. He says he loves that show and keeps chanting, "Netflix and chill." Katherine stares out my window, across the car park, as though she can't hear him, and I stare at a small water stain on the carpet.

A pregnant emptiness fills the room. Michael looks momentarily embarrassed and disappears again.

Katherine turns her attention back to me. "So, you *are* taking your medication properly? I don't want to have to make another report, Vincent. Or have to talk to your parents again."

"Yeah, yeah, yeah. You know full well I am. Hard not to take them when you people are inspecting our mouths like dentists every time after. It's not like in those old movies, can't hide the damn things underneath your tongue, spit them out later or something."

"Are you spitting them out?"

"No."

"Do you feel like you're watching a movie sometimes, Vincent? Like your life is a film?" Katherine asks. Her eyes sharpen to small points and flicker brightly as though she's seen something she wants to eat. A chocolate cake in a bakery shop window.

My face burns up. I don't know what to say. I let my eyes fall to the threadbare, slime-green carpeting. Focusing on the water stain and then the shoes on Katherine's feet. Pink Crocs. Ridiculous footwear for a health care professional. I wait for her to leave my room. She doesn't. She stands next to my bed as though she's waiting for a bus to take her somewhere far away.

"We have a group therapy session at 12:40 and then an art therapy session at 3 o'clock today, Vincent. I'd like it very much if you attended both," she says, suddenly perky— bouncing on the balls of her feet. Her breasts and stomach ripple slightly like crimson ocean water.

"Oh, wow, great, *art therapy*. The woman I love killed herself by jumping off a cliff thousands of miles away and it was all *my* fault. Painting a vase with shitty plastic roses stuck in it isn't going to make things any better, is it? Art therapy isn't therapeutic at all," I say, swallowing back the yells that gather at the back of my throat like the warm tea and stale toast they force us to eat an hour before "lights out." I tell myself not to get angry. Calm down. Control myself. What I need is a proper drink. A double shot of whiskey with two cubes of ice. Something to make the world a watercolor painting. Take the sharp edges away from the corners. Just something to relax me a little instead of the pills that rip the remnants of my soul out of me. The last time I had a proper drink, I tried to hang myself from the bathroom door. Not drunk since. If I ever made it to an AA meeting, they would've been proud of me. I could quit drinking easily. I only had to get hospitalized to do it.

"Yes, *that's* one of the very things that is important for us to *discuss*, Vincent. Could it be possible that you're avoiding the private sessions and talking about *Amelie,* because you're anxious about what may come from it? What you may come to realize?"

"No... No! I don't know what you're talking about. I have a migraine. I want to go back to sleep."

"Don't you know what I'm referring to, Vincent? Think about it a little and we'll talk about it more later. Okay?"

"Like I already said before, I have a really bad migraine. I just want to sleep." I raise my eyebrows at the open door, hoping she'll take the hint and piss off.

She doesn't. Still standing there, observing me, squinting through the thick lenses of her glasses for a long minute. Eyes like Pepsi bottle caps.

We look coolly at each other, blinking.

"Vincent, you have to help us to help you. Stop fighting your recovery."

"Stop fighting? It feels like I was knocked out a long time ago," I say lifting my arm, pressing the wristwatch Amelie gave me to my ear. The synchronicity of its ticking heartbeat soothes me. I close my eyes tight. Counting exhalations.

A picture grows in the darkness. Shapes take form. Colors bleed together.

Katherine is gone now.

This world fades away. I'm not there.

FOUR

Amelie is crying again.

Grasping a scrunched-up paper napkin to her eyes.

Face hidden.

Veiled.

I'm confused. Why is she weeping when I am the one in mourning?

It takes me a few seconds to realize where we are.

We're sitting in the rooftop bar of a hotel. Our hotel. Downtown Hanoi, Vietnam. Another trip we'd taken at the beginning of the second year of our relationship to outrun the sins we committed together. Amelie had always wanted to go to Vietnam. She said it was on her bucket list. I never had a bucket list. Amelie encouraged me to make one. "Death is our shadow, it's always there in our silhouette, my darling," she wrote in thick, black marker on my bedroom wall. It was the first thing my eyes woke up to in the mornings.

In the bar, the Hanoi heat is a migraine. Red rice-paper lanterns shaped like hearts hang twisted from the tin roof. I remember the way they dangled in the breeze before. They're motionless now. Static. The drink bar in the center of the place is unmanned and derelict.

A place for shadows and silhouettes.

I lick my lips. Dehydrated. The back of my skull throbs. Hungover. Hands palsied from too much whiskey the night before.

Or from the meds this morning.

I don't know.

A plate of French fries on the table between us. Uneaten. Cold. The empty mug with the cracked lip still screaming, **happy dayz**.

There's a taxidermy baby alligator standing on its hind legs, wearing a tiny top hat and grasping a small jar of toothpicks in front of its flaking stomach.

Everything is pale green, except for Amelie and me. And the sky. The sky is a child's crayon shade of blue. *Happy dayz.*

Amelie is beautiful even when she's crying. More beautiful, even. Wearing a tight halter top showing off her tits. Making me feel equally horny and possessive underneath the throbbing of my head. Her mobile phone screen-down in front of her as usual. It's vibrating. As usual. Over and over again like a heart attack. I don't know why I'm here again in this Hanoi hotel. Recently, I can't concentrate. The things I want to remember don't materialize. Negativity and regret play on repeat like elevator music. Recollecting the shitty moments best forgotten. The B-sides of our relationship.

I can't save Amelie here.

I'm chain-smoking. Lungs aching. I'm angry but can't remember why. Every so often, I drag my gaze from Amelie to glance over at the other buildings below. There's a squat Vietnamese woman hanging laundry from a clothesline on a rooftop. A green dress. A red sweater. Makes me think about gallows. I snub my cigarette out in an orange ashtray and shake the thoughts away.

The phone won't stop vibrating.

My eyes flow up and down Amelie's cleavage to her throat. She isn't wearing the diamond necklace I bought for her birthday. She'd ripped it from her neck mid-argument last night, tossed it over the balcony. I wonder if it's still at the bottom of the hotel pool or if some lucky kid discovered it like sunken treasure. The thick scent of chlorine. When I dive in later, searching for it, it'll be gone. Taken like so many other things.

"Looks as though someone's messaging you again, huh, Amelie?"

This is another repeat, my personal *Groundhog Day*, my chance to set things right, but I find myself saying the same things I said the first time.

She sniffs. Ignoring me. Scratching at the pink scars shaped like grins on her left arm.

"Who is it always messaging you anyway?" I try to snatch the phone, but she pulls it into her lap underneath the tabletop.

Greg, the support staffer from the ward, is sitting on a bar stool, strumming an acoustic guitar. He's dressed in emerald scrubs. A shit-eating grin slapped all over his greasy face. The tune is Elvis' "Can't Help Falling in Love." The small cardboard sign propped at his feet has **FOR TWO NIGHTS ONLY** scribbled in black marker pen.

"This prick's playing our song." I jerk my head in his direction.

"Only two nights," Amelie pouts.

I snatch an empty beer bottle from the table, make to throw it at Greg, but the bar stool is vacant now except for the piece of cardboard.

Only for two nights.

"I fucking hate this memory of us. Why am I here again? I hate it." I twist back around in my chair to face Amelie. Legs numb. Pins and needles. Short of breath. Sweating. I stink like I haven't washed for days. In the clinic, I haven't.

Amelie sobs again. Nodding into a fresh napkin she pulls from a chrome dispenser reflecting the sun. The taxidermy baby alligator is knocked to the floor. Toothpicks scatter. The thing grins up at me viciously, broken in half. "Me too. I don't like remembering this at all. It was like the fourth or fifth time we broke up. We shouldn't have always drunk so much," she says.

"Yeah, I know. We argued really bad about something last night. I can't even remember the reason now. Something about your phone. I left you alone in our room. Drank all night, here in the bar."

"You called me a selfish fucking bitch." She lets out another sob.

"Did I? I can't remember that at all." I shake my pounding head to try to convince myself more than her.

"You're only remembering what you want to remember again, Vincent. You always treated me like I was something disposable to you...and the baby." The word *disposable* comes out breathless and croaked. A mixture of bitterness and sadness soaked deep into the seams.

My throat is sore and very dry. I swallow something sharp. Jagged. Words tumble out of my mouth like broken teeth falling onto the tabletop. A recently recurring theme. I think I heard somewhere that losing your teeth in a dream means you're stressed. This isn't a dream though, it's a memory.

No, it's not. It's a cheap imitation of the past.

"That's not true, Amelie. You always turned your shit back onto me. Now you're trying to make me suffer for it. No one's still blowing up *my* phone." I pat myself down for my phone. It isn't there. I don't know where it is. We aren't allowed personal phones in the clinic. It's another one of their rules.

"It *is* true, Vincent. You always pushed me away. You treated me like some kind of sex friend, a fuck buddy, but went crazy any time I even spoke to anybody else. Go to our last time together. That was crazy. Really fucking crazy. Replay that little memory. You'll see."

"No! And that time was your fault, too. Not just mine."

"Why not? You don't even want to remember, do you? Because you know. That's why, isn't it, Vin?"

"I don't want to go there again."

"Yeah, I thought as much." She shrugs, drops the napkin to the floor. Her face blurs, featureless.

"I'm going to Margate, the lighthouse. I'm going to find you there. I can change it."

Amelie sobs harder, pulling a fresh napkin from the dispenser. The dispenser is an Art Deco orange plastic now.

"Will you please stop crying, Amelie?"

"No, I can't."

"Why?"

"Because I didn't stop crying when we were in this place the first time. In a moment, I'll get up and leave you here. I'll go back down to our room, pack my things, and catch a taxi to the airport. I didn't stop crying the whole time. I won't stop crying now. See! That's what you need to understand. You can't change a photograph, Vincent. No matter how hard you squint your eyes and tell yourself you're meditating. The past is the past. It's done. I'm going to the airport. I don't stop crying. That's it."

"I remember," I say. "We'll meet again in front of the departure gate. We ignored each other the whole flight home. It was awkward as hell."

We catch each other's eyes and smile. It's as though Amelie is still alive.

"Yeah, so stupid. And it was such a nice trip, too. Until the last night." She grins.

"Yeah, maybe you should have switched off your phone. Given us a chance to fix things."

"Maybe you shouldn't have been so jealous and so fucking possessive all the time."

"You fucked someone else, Amelie. And you're still texting them."

She hides her face behind the napkin again. "I'm not! You're being a paranoid weirdo again. Anyway, I thought we were broken up. I was hurt and lonely. You broke up with me! What was I supposed to do?"

"You weren't supposed to fuck the first guy you met."

"Don't play it all high and mighty like you never cheated on me. You think I'm dumb. I know you've cheated."

"I can swear on my life that I've never cheated on you."

"Oh, the manic-fucking-depressant is swearing on his life now…"

"I would never cheat on you because I'd never want to hurt you."

"You hurt me in the worst way there is."

"So you fucked another guy to get back at me?"

She lists her excuses in monotone. "No, I was mentally ill. I was depressed. I needed someone to talk to. He took advantage of me. I was lonely. I was drunk. It was only for two nights! It meant nothing. I want you. I only ever wanted you. I'm dead, Vincent. I'm fucking dead, stop punishing me."

The plate of French fries has changed somehow into a bowl of pistachios. A fly crawls over the bloody teeth mixed in with the shells. I push the bowl away from me. "Look, all right, the mistakes don't matter now. I don't want to argue about the past anymore, I want to change it."

Amelie pulls the napkin away from her face. There are crusty salt trails on her cheeks. She laughs bitterly. "But you can't."

"Why?"

"I already told you why. You can't change a memory, Vin. All this!" She waves her arms around the bar. "All of this has already happened. You can't change what's already been done."

"I want to try. Let's try, Amelie. I want to. I need to. I don't want to lose you again." My voice breaks. "We can at least try, Amelie. Can't we? I want to try to change it all."

"No, I said we can't. It's done. Fucking finished. Over."

The word *over* hits me in the face like falling headfirst into concrete. A blurring pain behind my eyeballs. The air shimmers. "Why are you being such a selfish fucking bitch, Amelie?"

"See!" she wails. Placing both hands to her face. Fingers trembling.

I feel cold and hard inside my stomach. Losing her again.

As a child, I witnessed an old woman get killed by a truck. I remember her hair was very white. She stepped off the curb into traffic. She was wearing a pale green coat and had a blue plastic bag full of oranges clasped in her left hand. One of the oranges rolled passed me on the street. Small splashes of red on it.

In some cultures, oranges are a symbol of fertility. Pregnancy. Birth. Babies.

I'm making all the same mistakes over and over.

My guts all tangled. Blocked up. Itching like fresh petrol burns. I have internal bleeding. I need to take a shit. Trying to speak; nothing comes out from my lips. The words aborted and swallowed back down to poison. Part of me knows Amelie isn't even here in Hanoi and neither am I. It's the part of myself I want to kill the most.

She pushes her chair out to leave. The legs dragging across tile dully echo. I grab weakly at her wrist, my hand passing through her like a cloud of cigarette smoke. She walks away from the table. She always walks away first. It's the first few steps in the dance we perform. Shadows slow dancing in derelict rooms.

Pulling away. Splitting. Detaching. Discarding. Painting black. Relapsing. Reengaging. Repeating. Recycling. Reincarnating. Love bombing. Pulling away. Splitting. Detaching. Discarding. Painting black.

She doesn't glance back. Ever. I've already lived this all a thousand times. Still committing the same offenses. Over and over again like a film on repeat in an isolated theater or a doctor's waiting room. Like these words. These thoughts. My inner monologues.

Guilt is Limbo on a loop.

I flick my cigarette off the roof and watch it fall, spin to the gray, cracked, moped-infested concrete below. Light another smoke, listen to the diminishing sound of Amelie's high heels on hard flooring as I stare out over the silent morning city.

The elderly woman is still hanging out her washing. Frozen in place. The elevator in the hallway chimes as it opens then closes, swallowing my heart and everything the arteries connect it to. Amelie. Noticing cars and pedestrians stuck in time, identical to the ancient washerwoman. This is all simply a painted backdrop. I drag deeply on the cigarette. It tastes of nothing. Not even air.

I open my eyes. I'm holding two unfilled fingers to my lips, sitting on my bed. The tips of the fingers stained a milk-coffee brown and stinking. The gray light of day still leaking, shredded, through my chicken-wire glass windows.

I'm alone.

Back in my room. Back in the clinic. Not in New Jersey. Not in Hanoi. London. Limbo. Where all love goes to die. There's a mansion of derelict rooms living inside me. A cancer ward for dissatisfaction. A life support system for comatose regrets. A crumbling morgue of happier, better times. A rain-drenched grave for the past.

FIVE

Afternoon.

Group therapy time.

We're all slumped on recliners in a large circle. The inpatients. 12 of us. Roman numerals on a broken clock face. Bath robes and dressing gowns wrapped tightly around bodies make it seem as though we're relaxing poolside at a five-star hotel. Only the spasms and the trembling of our limbs give us away.

A pick and mix of ages and mental illnesses. Disorders. Most are self-harmers or failed suicide attempts. Some stare. Some hang their heads. Most fidget, scratch and pick at themselves. Take your choice of any mental health stereotype on the big screen and they're here. The whole happy mental health family together.

Group therapy is situated in the common room. There's nothing common about any of it. Walls painted a burnt orange and peeling like dead skin at the corners. The recliners are the garden center, Home Depot variety. Cheap plastic. Some are white and some are olive green. The room is a New Year's Day kind of cold.

A woman strikingly similar to Amelie beams from a creased poster partly taped over a crack. Teaching 10 ways to improve wellbeing. Another poster by the door has a color-coded graph with Amelie again. She's counting down the five stages of loss on her fingertips. I stare at her green nail varnish, wondering where I'm currently at in the scheme of things.

Denial.

Anger.

Bargaining.

Depression.

Acceptance.

The first word makes my stomach roll. I don't know why. I guess I'm at number four on the list. Depression. I stare at the poster until I go cross-eyed. Rub at my eyelids, blink, and the girl isn't Amelie anymore. She's just a nondescript white model, the kind fake smiling from faded posters in hospitals and clinics anywhere in the world. I look away, taking another long glance around the room and the people I'm surrounded by. Distraction is key when I'm faced with these kinds of situations.

A chunky, old-fashioned television set usually showing old detergent commercials and cartoons is screwed into an iron bracket on the wall. It's switched off now. Its ink-black glass casts hellish reflections from its vacant, idiot screen. The stand-by light flashing red—a time bomb waiting to blow us all to bloody pulp. I glance at my wristwatch and wish it would fucking go off already.

The torn sofas and the worn-out billiard table have been pushed back against the far windows. The wooden cues and balls are under lock and key in the main office. I used to enjoy playing billiards but have never seen anyone else playing. It's difficult to enjoy anything here. I wonder if you could kill yourself with an 8 ball.

A portable stereo balanced on a smaller plastic picnic table plays a CD of birdsong. "Bird Songs of Britain - The Sunset Chorus - Nature Sounds for Relaxation, Meditation, Visualisation & Sleep!" the case said when I scrutinized it once. I'd like to tell Katherine that listening to birds squawking, like the clinic's panpipe pop covers, isn't therapeutic, and it just makes the place sound like a damn aviary, but I don't because in group therapy I try to avoid attention at all costs.

She's perched on a tall stool in the middle of us. Moaning her way through her little notebook of relaxation hymns, a priest who has lost faith and renounces God, but preaches anyway because it's a job. A paycheck. A way to survive. Katherine probably thinks she's Jesus Christ and we're all her rotting lepers, begging her to cure us. Make us clean. Righteous. Normal.

Jesus, protect me…

I'm staring at the black-and-white collar of a priest. A plastic Bart Simpson keyring I got from Santa Claus clutched in my small, moist hand. I'm eight years old.

My eyes are sore. I've been crying. It's my grandmother's wake. There's so much sadness in her house, it's dripping down the damp walls.

I'm telling the priest I can sometimes see death. The priest's name is Mr. White. He plays guitar and sings religious songs in my school gymnasium during Easter and Christmas assemblies. He asks me what I think death looks like. He has a small smile on his face, a very red neck, and keeps pulling at the collar around his throat like the belt of colorful beads calling to me from a drawer in my bedroom at home. I tell him death is black scribble on a crumpled piece of paper and I see it in my head when I can't sleep at night. He tells me to ask Jesus to protect me if I feel afraid of the dark. I tell him I'm not afraid. The black scribble is beautiful. His eyebrows are thick and hairy and jump around on his forehead like small dogs. He tells me to pray to Jesus anyway, Jesus will always protect me, and Jesus died for all my sins.

I get up and walk away from him. Even at eight years old, I know when I'm being lied to.

The only thing Jesus ever taught me was how to die.

Katherine is another fraud that doesn't know what she's talking about.

"Imagine an ocean. The waves passing softly over the sandy beach. Imagine a river running through a lush, green forest. Imagine a darkened theater with an empty screen. Imagine all the stress and worry drifting up through your body and out the top of your head. And…relax…relax…relax…" She drones on and on.

I close my eyes for a few minutes, and then open them, peeking at the other patients to see if they're buying this bullshit. They look like drowned corpses stretched out on autopsy tables. Katherine still yammering.

Beatrice, an attractive English-Italian painter who I heard tried to gas herself, peeks back at me, winks and lifts her hand from the arm of her recliner to give me a little wave.

She came to the clinic a week after me. We've never said more than 50 words in passing, though there seems to be a kind of nodded mutual respect. The kind of respect two people can only reach once they've tried to kill themselves and failed. I like the atmosphere Beatrice constantly has around her. Her body language shouting that she's just a tourist here. An observer. She doesn't intend on sticking around too long. Some stars are just meant to go supernova.

She's blonde, beautiful, fucked up (obviously), and likes to shout the word "fuck" at people a lot. In a different life, before Amelie, she would've been exactly my type. Maybe, she even reminds me a little of her. I don't really know anymore. I see Amelie everywhere. In everyone. In everything. *Does that mean I'm still on the denial part of the five stages of grief?*

I attempt a smile, give Beatrice a small wave back. She smirks as though we're sharing a private joke, laughing with her eyes the way Amelie used to and then closing them. I watch her body unclamp, sink further into the recliner, and relax. Katherine's spiel seemingly working in ways it doesn't for me. She has a good body. I glance at the poster of the girl who looks like Amelie again.

Scotty, the guy who has been in the clinic longer than anyone else, is snoring. Noises like paper slowly ripped down the center. A letter torn up. A Dear John. An ultrasound printout with a fuzzy black-and-white picture of a 10-week-old child who might've been but never was.

A suicide note.

My thoughts are stuck now. Feeling completely hollow, like I'm standing in an elevator that's going down too fast. I flinch and pick at the scratched and scarred armrest of the plastic recliner. Squeezing my eyes shut, I try to follow Katherine's voice as though it's a trail of blood out of a bad hangover fog.

Katherine tells us to go to our happy places in that voice completely devoid of emotion. Making me feel nauseous as though I'm gripping a phone to my ear, listening to a robot tell me the number I've called is no longer available.

The number you have dialed is temporarily unavailable, please try again later. The number you have dialed is temporarily unavailable, please try again later. The number you have dialed is temporarily unavailable, please try again later.

Blocked.

Stuck.

Amelie is dead.

I am a ghost.

I squeeze the armrests of the chair until my knuckles crack. At the top of a rusty rollercoaster. A South End theme park by the beach. Alton Towers. Chessington World of Adventure.

Now I'm an eight-year-old child again in piss-drenched denim dungarees.

The tobacco-stained ceiling of the common room spins wildly. A spinning, cracked plate balanced on a stick gripped in the dirty hand of a grinning, grease-painted clown with running makeup.

Now I age. Grow older. No longer a scared kid, I'm a scared adult. Full of gray rainwater and shit. I squeeze my eyes closed again, try to focus on something that had been good. The happy place Katherine is mumbling on about. I fumble through time and space, grasping and snatching at flashing memories like a deck of cards tossed into the air. I'm the king of hearts. The suicide king.

I close my eyes tightly. The muscles in my cheeks spasm.

A warm spreading darkness, expanding. Dilating. Merging with a rich amber. Flecks of gold scattered throughout cosmos. A liquid Milky Way.

Then eyelashes—long, curled, jet black.

An eyebrow—chestnut brown. Arched in amusement.

Peroxide-blonde hair spread over a red-and-green tartan blanket.

A cheek, high-boned. Almost regal.

The small, chocolate-colored mole Amelie always fingers when nervous.

Down to the tips of full, pink lips. Pushed out by slightly crooked teeth. Lips that whisper the words "I love you" many times and will, two years from this moment, scream the final, "Fuck you." But this is now, and the lips are smiling. I'm smiling.

Happy.

This is a good memory.

This is one of my happy places. Not the happiest, but one of them.

Hyde Park in July.

A Wednesday afternoon, our first year together. Many months before our trip to Vietnam. Before the murder. Before the damage was done.

Amelie and I called in sick for work this morning. Hoping to get the Summer Park to ourselves. Except for the occasional dog-walker or jogger, we are alone.

Lying underneath an ancient oak tree. An empty bottle of red wine next to a half-drunk bottle of white. An unopened pack of paper cups on the recently mown grass next to us. Crumpled sandwich wrappers. The air is bathwater warm. Traffic in the distance comes in waves—an ocean's surf passing over wet, gritty sand. Insects hum. Birds sing as though in contest. Sounds as though we're in an aviary, but we aren't, we're in a happier time.

One of the happy places Katherine told me to go to.

I prop myself on an elbow and kiss Amelie. She tastes like wine and late summertime moistened by rain.

Happy dayz.

We take our time with each other. Softly at first, working our way up. Then deeper, harder. Her tongue hot, sliding over mine, teasingly flickering in and out of my mouth. Lost in the senses of each other. I run my hand up her thigh, over the smooth skin, leisurely, savoring it, and underneath the smooth fabric of her denim skirt. Fingers sliding over her cotton panties. Early morning dew. Inhaling her breath down into my lungs as it leaves her lips in short, aching sighs. Exploring lands that I've conquered hundreds of times. Places I've made my home. She's caressing the front of my jeans with one hand and my jaw with the other. Hurried now and eager. Of all the things she does to make me crazy, it's her hands on my face that lingers long after I'm alone with myself. I don't know why. Her face and eyes always desperately seeking out mine. The neediness in it. A sensation, how, I imagine, it must feel to have a beautiful ghost pass by you in a crowded room. Tracing its fingers across your neck and throat. Something supernaturally frightening but mesmerizing.

I break away a moment to quickly gaze around the perimeter of the park. A few people on the other side of the pond lazily kick a football back and forth, but there's no one else. I grin at her. She knows what I'm thinking. She always does. She grins back. Mirroring my actions. My emotions. Something she's done since we first met. I only noticed after she was gone.

"Again?" she giggles faux-shy, faux-shocked.

Dopamine floods my brain in cloudy waves. A tsunami of it.

"We already did it twice this morning, Vin."

"Yeah, but that was this morning and it's the afternoon now." I playfully lick her lips, ease myself on top of her. Biting her neck, kissing her shoulder, the way I know makes her feral. Her breasts pressed against my chest. Her heartbeat. She writhes under me like water, uncontrollably aflame. Working my free hand up her trembling thigh again, underneath her skirt and pulling aside her panties. Sliding a finger over the short, wiry hairs and deeply into the swollen folds of her.

"Here?! No way! Are you crazy?!" she pants the words, shudders, arching her back off the ground. Pushing herself harder into me.

"Yeah, right here," I say, teasing her with curled fingers, causing an ecstatic spasm to ripple through her.

"We'll get into so much trouble if we're caught, Vincent," she whispers, but she's fumbling, unbuttoning my jeans, pushing down the waistband of my shorts and pulling me forcefully closer. I pull aside her panties until I hear the cotton tear. She gasps. Kissing my mouth harder. Opening up to me. A door not slammed shut but thrown wide open. She lets out a stifled moan as I slide myself into her. Closer, tighter, deeper. Both hurried and slowed. Rushed and concentrated. Pained and pleasured. Amelie says we fuck how we love, and she's right. We always fuck like we are dying after the act. Killing each other softly. And we are. Killing each other. But it isn't a quick death. It's terminally beautiful, all-encompassing, and fatal. It's the small deaths that make up life. Everything else is just time-filler and commercial breaks. We're arsonists burning each other down to ash and cinders. To nothing.

Orgasm comes in bucking throes, like jumping into the cool ocean from the end of a pier when I was 15 and truly believed I was immortal.

This July day in Hyde Park is one of the times I travel to most when I'm shuffling around in pharmaceutical circles. Dozing off in the common room. The clinic. I try to force my mind to the place she died. The lighthouse. The cliffs. I want to save her. It's hard to recollect a time and a place if you were never there. This memory of the park is a time when the woman I loved, loved me. That's all you need in life. For someone to breathlessly whisper your name in the heat of the summer sun. In the shadows of the night, for someone to pull you inside them and let you live there. Die there. To want you there. Need you there.

After, we both lie sprawled, squinting up at the ocean-colored sky, breathless, satisfied. Comfortable. Amelie pulls the sunglasses from my face as soon as I put them on and slips them over her own eyes. She sighs. Pecks my cheek three times and turns my jaw to her. I can see my reflection in the dark lenses of the Wayfarers. I close my eyes. Lie back down.

"That was so, so good. I love it when you don't wear a condom. When you come inside me. Does that make me sound like a slut or something?"

"No, not at all. I like it, too. To be honest, a rubber was the last thing on my mind anyway. Besides, you're on the pill, right?" I say it to the clouds and then roll onto my side to gaze at her when she doesn't answer me. Search for reassurance in her features but find none there. Just my own pale face in the dark lenses once more.

Amelie is looking down at the blanket, grinning. To herself more than to me. A strange smile she lets slip sometimes. A beautiful kind of spiteful. An off-color joke that only she knows the punchline to. Whenever I glimpse it, I feel as though I'm walking a rope pulled taut. Miles above the concrete with jeering, ugly crowds below. A tightrope for me alone. Vertigo, a noose around my throat. She slips a knife beneath my ribs and congratulates herself.

"You told me you were on the pill. You are on the pill, right, Amelie?" I'm choked even by the idea of having a screaming, weeping child when I'm already drowning in debt and struggling to make ends meet living in my dilapidated, cramped apartment. I don't want a child. I'd probably be a complete piece of shit father anyway.

"Yeah, yeah, yeah." She flashes that blade-like smile again then puffs up her cheeks, blowing out an exacerbated breath. "Don't be so fucking insecure all the time. The pill, the pill, the pill. I'm on the fucking pill, okay? Sometimes, I think that's all you give a shit about, Vin. What's the matter, you don't want to have a baby with me or what? You hate the thought of having a child with me, is that it? I'm not good enough to be a mother? I thought you were serious about me, Vincent?"

I clear my throat, hesitate, and Amelie sits up on the blanket, crossing her legs the way we sat in school assembly as eight-year-olds. Hitching down her skirt to cover her thighs. Self-conscious now. Hair wild, hanging in her face, catching the sun like fool's gold. Even at times like this, she's stunningly beautiful. Maybe more so. And I want her more. Need her more.

I sit up, too. I feel it's expected now.

The atmosphere shifts. The landscape darkens. In the sky, a rainstorm grows like an illness. Thick, black clouds metastasizing, swelling a deep purple. The back of my neck itches. Skin raw. Fiction-burns from a cord around my throat.

When I was eight years old, I hung myself. 20 years later, I did it again.

This is limbo.

A memory within a dream within a memory dreamed by a very ill man in a hospital ward.

I glance around the park again and notice the trees have all died. Only leafless, rotten, grotesque black sculptures remain. The grass has yellowed. Desolation crawls wounded, twitching over everything. I gag on the stench of rot and cleaning products.

This isn't one of my happy places anymore. I already know what's next. Amelie pushes me. Slaps my face. I rock back and forth.

"Well, fucking say something. You don't want a baby with me or what?" She grimaces.

I should end things here, but I don't. The sex is too good. The poisonous parts of the relationship are too toxically addictive. I don't want to be alone with myself. I don't know what to say, so I do what I always do and lie to her. "Sure, I do, but not right now. I am serious about you, but you know—it's complicated."

"You fucking liar. You're not serious with me at all."

"I am serious with you. Why do you have to rush things? We've only been dating for what? A year? If that. Amelie? We haven't even…met each other's friends and families…and all that other kind of bullshit."

"Oh, meeting my mother is bullshit, now, is it?"

"What? No! No way! What the hell are you talking about? I meant meeting *my* friends and my family, that's all."

"I haven't met any of your friends and family because I'm just your friend with benefits, right? The girl you're using to get over the last bitch, right?"

"No, no, not at all. I've told my friends about you."

"You don't even have any friends."

"Well, neither do you, but that's not really the point I was trying to get at here."

"I do have friends, back home, in Jersey. They'd like you a lot. I've told them all about you."

"What are we even talking about here? You're only 23. I'm 26. We're still young. You don't want to be tied down with a kid now, surely?"

"Do you love me or don't you, Vincent?" She's plucking at strands of grass. Yanking them out of the ground and tossing them away. Realities shift. For a second, I'm back in the clinic common room, watching one of the other patients: a young woman called Mandy, pulling out handfuls of her hair and dropping them to the scuffed tile. Looking up and off to the right, avoiding eye contact. She gags. Dry heaves. Blurts out that she thinks she has morning sickness. I quickly turn back to Amelie. Concentrating on the past.

"Yes, you know I do, Amelie."

"So why do you hate the idea of having a baby with me? Is it such an awful fucking idea? Now is as good a time as any, isn't it? I would be a good mom; I know I would." Her voice breaks. A tear slides down her face and drops onto her skirt, making a small dark stain in the stonewashed denim. She rubs at her stomach as though there's already a baby kicking inside.

"I don't hate the idea and it isn't awful at all. I think you would be an awesome mother. I just think now isn't a great time. I told you, it's complicated. And we'll need money."

"What's money got to do with anything? If you really loved me, you'd want a baby with me."

"We'll need money for baby stuff. A crib. Baby clothes. Nappies. Stuff like that. I don't know. Come on, we still hardly know each other?" As soon as I say the last few words, I know it's a mistake. But I feel pushed into a corner. Like I need to negotiate.

"What the fuck?! After a fucking year together and you telling me you love me?!" She grabs up a plastic cup to throw a drink in my face but realizes it's empty and lets it roll from her hand onto the blanket.

I stutter and fumble at words, attempting to save a situation that's already lost. "I just mean, we are still getting to know each other. Learning about each other. I want to know everything about you. Maybe even start living together, you know? Get a place together first. That kind of stuff. Renew your visa."

"This is about your ex, isn't it?! You're still in love with her, aren't you? You've just been using me this whole time!?"

"What? No! I haven't spoken to her since I met you."

"I bet you're still texting her, aren't you? Show me your phone!" She snatches my mobile phone from the blanket and searches through it for a few minutes and then tosses it back into my lap. She bites her bottom lip. Looks disappointed.

"Are we going to go through each other's phones now?"

She quickly pushes her mobile phone into her bag, "I just don't understand what you want. I want a future with you. I want a baby with you. You said we were like soulmates. What was that? Bullshit conversation so you could fuck me? You're so full of shit, Vincent!"

"I did? When did I say that?"

"The very first night we met. You can't even remember? You were probably drunk then too."

"What? No!"

"You're always fucking drunk nowadays. I gave up so much for you already, Vincent. I gave up my life in America for you! I had a fiancé."

"What? You told me he treated you like shit. Said he was abusive."

"I never said that. Ever! Fuck this and fuck you! I'm going home."

"No, Amelie, don't. Wait. Let's talk properly about this. All right?"

"No, this is bullshit. You're such a shitty person, Vincent. You just want to use me all the time. Your little American piece on the side, right? The only time you ever wanna meet is when you wanna fuck! You're a piece of shit and so am I. Everything is shit. Shit! Shit! Shit! Just fuck off, Vincent."

I sit there on the ground, stuttering out words and watching her storm off across the park. That was all I ever did.

All I ever do.

Watch her walk away.

Watch her leave me.

Split. Detach. Discard. Paint black. Relapse. Reengage. Repeat. Recycle.

I knew our fight was a massive red flag, one of many, but I found that the more uncontrollable Amelie became, the more hooked I got. I couldn't go back to what my life was like before her. My old life drowned the very first moment I saw her. Her love was a cuckoo in the nest of my mind. There was space for nothing else. Our relationship became a heroin rush. Crackhead love.

Once, halfway through a third bottle of wine, Amelie told me she thought real love was like running a razorblade across your arm in front of the bathroom mirror. Watching the blood pour over the white porcelain. Dripping raindrops the color of life. The pain pulsing like an orgasm. She said love washed us clean. Made us pure again. I didn't know what she meant. I put it down to the drink. But I came to understand. I really did.

In the vacuum of the park, I lie back on the blanket and close my eyes, waiting for her to come back.

Another thing I was always doing.

I'm always doing.

Waiting for her to come back to me. After she walked away. After she was gone.

Amelie disappeared for days after our fight in the park.

Her phone switched off. I never found out where she went or who she was with. She showed up one night at my apartment, sullen, apologetic, and clingy. Bruises on her thighs and upper arms. Dripping out information in a maddening trickle. She'd been with friends. Then the story changed. She'd gone to visit an uncle who lived in Oxford. Then it wasn't an uncle, it was a co-worker. Became hysterical anytime I asked where she'd really been. Questioned who she'd really been with. She screamed at me until the neighbors started banging on the walls. Said I was a horrible person for trying to get her to admit to something she hadn't done. I was told to stop fucking interrogating her like a cop. I was being delusional. Paranoid.

The questions were making her crazy. I was told to just fucking drop it. It was none of my business because we were on a break. It was a break I'd known nothing about. She hid her mobile phone from me or turned it face-down. She'd let it ring itself out. She started self-harming every time the subject was brought up. Carving long gashes on her wrists with whatever pointed objects were closest at hand.

I stopped asking questions. I shut up. I heard the threat of suicide so many times, it became part of our relationship. Another lover sleeping between us in the night. Its vacuous eyes staring blankly at me as I lay, unseeing in the dark.

Now stop.

Skip forward to her birthday two months later.

Amelie and I fixed things. Had been getting along better. I thought. I bought her a diamond necklace she wanted. Surprising her at home with it. She was reluctant to let me into her bedroom. Said she'd been sleeping. It felt weird. I glimpsed subtle attempts to push her mobile phone under a couch pillow. Something like a block of ice in my guts, I snatched the phone from her. She shrieked and clawed at me. Messages from some other guy on the cracked screen. Wrote she was **a lot of fun**. He couldn't wait to meet her again. I asked her if she'd fucked him. Waving the phone in front of her face. She yelled at me to calm the fuck down. He was just a friend. She stuttered. He lived in another country. She avoided eye contact. It was nothing. Just text messages. I was paranoid again. Completely overreacting. I needed help. I had trust issues. Was I drinking too much again? She said I was all she needed.

Days passed. I refused to let it go. Truth trickled out. They'd been sending sexual messages to each other. But that was all. Nothing else. My guts felt cancerous with a constant boiling suspicion. I told her we were over. Fucking finished. Called her a selfish bitch. She said I was throwing her away. I was a monster. I was a psychopath. She smashed the living room windows in my apartment with her stilettos. Scratched her initials into my front door with the spare key and then posted it through the letterbox.

Days passed. Hundreds of missed calls on my phone. When I finally gave in and answered, she told she'd been diagnosed with cervical cancer. I ran to her place, pulled her into my arms. Bloody tissues littered her room. Jagged incisions tattooed her forearms. Later, she said it was a mistake, a misdiagnosis. There was no cancer. I was relieved. Later still, she admitted she'd lied, but only because she couldn't live without me. She begged. Threatened suicide again. She needed me. I stayed. I forgave her. My guts continued to scream. I dreamt of crocodiles every single time I drifted off to sleep. I questioned my sanity. Walked on eggshells. Broken glass. I didn't know what was truth and what was fabrication. I loved her.

I love her still.

I can't explain what our relationship was. It was symbiotic. It was a death dance. Nothing is sweeter than the pleasurable pain inflicted from a beautiful woman who licks the blood away from your flesh after she's wounded you.

My eyes close. The sickly yellow light burns through my eyelids, creating murky shapes. A kaleidoscope of shard-like images from the past.

Someone gently shakes my shoulder. I snap my eyes open, expecting to see Amelie silhouetted by a gray sky and the rotten greenery of the park.

I already know she doesn't come back. I've been to that place many times before.

The park. What starts a happy memory. But I can never change the unhappy ending.

My shoulder is shaken again. Harder. Impatiently.

SIX

My eyes snap open. Focus. Clear. The setting sun of memory fades into another kind of delusion. One much darker. Less real.

It's not Amelie standing over me, but Beatrice silhouetted by the dull-flame orange, the drab interior of the common room. All the other recliners unoccupied. The room feels abandoned. Derelict. A crime scene of a murder at the very heart of the present.

"You snore louder than Scotty, you know?" Beatrice inhales deeply on a licorice paper roll-up, one eye squinted to the silver-blue smoke. I rub crust from my eyes, glimpsing two raw-pink, long scars on her creamy left wrist. Vertical cuts—not horizontal. Dirty blonde hair tied-up in a haphazard bun atop her head. A face of contradictions. Curdled milk pale but amused. Anxious but confident. Content and tormented. She pulls irritably at the wrinkled, faded black Rolling Stones T-shirt draped over her waif frame, slowly exhaling smoke out of her nostrils with an interested detachment. Her blue eyes gazing down on me with an even cooler interest, as though I'm a blank canvas she's contemplating painting. I realize I'm staring at her breasts and quickly look away, up at the clock on the far end wall above the door. Its battery ran out months ago. It always reads four minutes past eight. Eight. Four. August fourth. The day of Amelie's abortion. The clock a snide cosmic joke played on me by the Gods.

"I wasn't sleeping," I mumble dumbly.

"You're the one suffering delusions, yes? Like the painter Louis Wain. He painted cats smoking cigars and playing cards and other weird shit like that. He died in a mental hospital in Hertfordshire, I think. You know him?" She smiles kindly. Pityingly. Coffee-stained teeth and lips an oxygen-deprived light blue.

"You're the one who tried to gas herself like the poet Sylvia Plath. You know her?" The spite foaming at the corners of my mouth like dehydration feels sharply pleasurable. I don't know why.

Beatrice snorts in disgust and turns on the heels of her bare feet to leave.

I regret my words. Feel completely hollow. A sudden kind of dread. As though I'm a character in a cheap paperback novel about poltergeists.

I've been dead since the day I tied the cotton cord to the top of the bathroom door, knotted it around my throat, and tried to hang myself. I just don't know it yet. The realization will come much later, like the twist ending to a movie I've slept through.

I don't want Beatrice to walk away from me. Abandon me. Don't want to be left alone in this room with all its chairs standing vacant like ice statues of angels. "Wait up! Beatrice. Let me walk with you a little."

She stops, drops her cigarette onto the floor, steps on it, grinding it into the sticky, tiled flooring with the sole of her left foot. If it hurts, she shows no sign of it. "Well, okay, but I don't want to fucking talk about anything, all right?" she says, juggling a pouch of Golden Virginia Tobacco and some brown papers as she rolls another smoke.

"Fine by me," I mutter. "No *fucking* talking. I've got nothing much to say about anything anyway."

We do talk though. We talk a lot. About small things, mostly. Where we grew up. Schools. Families. Jobs we worked. Places we've been. All that kind of shit. Nothing too heavy. Nothing about what might've brought us to a mental clinic on the edge of a quiet North London town, where we can only leave on very special occasions and under constant supervision. Buzzed in and out by a bored, sparrow-like nurse named Davina. We tell each other as much as we tell ourselves, it's not a *proper* mental hospital. It's a clinic. There's a big difference. We're not proper mental cases.

So, Beatrice and I small talk. That *getting to know you* kind of small talk. Sitting together in the shade on a wobbly bench in the courtyard with its emaciated rose garden, yammering away at each other until one of the staff strolls through the halls of the clinic, ringing the lunch bell like the end of the world is nigh.

The End.

We snub out our cigarettes in a flowerpot full of sand and butts, both sighing satisfied as though we've just finished a three-course meal or fucked. Just two normal people passing the time, shooting the shit. For a moment, we can forget where we are, all the things that have made us who we are. Forget what brought us to the clinic in the first place. It's a beautiful fugue state of momentary contentment. Peace. Beatrice didn't try to gas herself in the garage of her South London home. I didn't try to hang myself with the cord off a pair of jogging bottoms from the bathroom door in my moldy, little apartment.

We are happy, healthy, shiny people. For a little while. Almost normal.

"You know what?" Beatrice says, slapping my chest with the back of her hand.

"What?" I ask.

"I was two completely different people in my dream last night. But both were cowards. What do you think about that?"

"Did you eat cheese with your toast and tea last night?" I glance at my wristwatch, decide I have time to light another cigarette and enjoy the random flow of Beatrice's conversation.

"No, why?"

"Cheese, you know, some people say if you eat cheese before you go to sleep, it gives you fucked up dreams. I don't know if it's true or not. Just what I heard."

She frowns, thinking it over, "No. No cheese. Okay, well, how about this? Do you ever dream of people that you've never met, so it's literally your mind that makes up their features? Makes up their voices and the things they say. It's so fucking weird when that happens to me."

My heart skips beats. A coronary coughing fit.

She slaps me on the back as though I'm choking to death.

"I don't really know what you mean. I used to dream about crocodiles a lot, though," I splutter.

"What were the crocs doing?"

"In my dreams?"

"No, at the *zoo*, arsehole," she says, playfully slapping me on the arm. "Of course in the *dreams*. You know, if you dream about a crocodile chasing you, it means you're going to be very successful. Were they chasing you, Vincent?"

"No, not chasing. They were hiding in the water and attacking me. Tearing chunks away from my arms and legs underneath the water. Fucked up, right? I might've watched too much of the Nature Channel."

Beatrice seems interested. Nodding her head with a concerned expression. "Crocodile attacks in zee dreams, zey symbolize betrayal," she puts on a bad Freudian accent.

"Really? Betrayal? I see." My heart goes into fits again.

She continues with the bad Austrian accent, "Yes, zat is quite correct. You see, zee crocodiles, zey symbolize zee hidden dangers of being betrayed. Zee crocodile, it is submerged malevolence. Zey lies. Do you see? Were you betrayed?"

I ignore the question, pretend I don't hear it and ask my own. "So, what the hell do *your* weird dreams mean then, dream expert?"

"I don't know. They *are* weird though, right? Just ignore me. Sometimes I say a lot of fucked up things for no reason. Verbal diarrhea, my dad used to say. By the way, before we go back inside, I want you to tell me all about your happy place, Vincent. What did you think about in there?" She nods back in the direction of the common room. A long strand of blonde hair falls out of the tightly wrapped bun, and she blows it out of her face. "In there. I want to know."

"My happy place? You really want to know?" I tightly pull my bathrobe together, like I'm cold but I'm not.

"Yeah, of course I want to know, that's why I asked, arsehole. I imagine it's somewhere exotic for some reason. Like Hawaii. I see palm trees, sand, and the ocean."

"Why do you keep calling me arsehole?"

"Maybe it's just my way of passively aggressive flirting with you." She inhales on her roll-up and her cheeks slightly flush.

"You *do* talk a lot of shite, Beatrice."

"Maybe you're right. Anyway, Hawaii? Palm trees? Beaches? Enlighten me, would you?"

"Yeah, sounds like one of my happy places, I guess. I have a few, actually."

"A few happy places? Aren't you a lucky boy then? Tell me where you went today."

I tell her. Describing every detail as though I'm in the park again. With Amelie. When I'm done, I snub out my cigarette, light another, and stare straight ahead, waiting for Beatrice to say something. It feels as though I'm stark naked. I pull the bathrobe around myself again.

Beatrice sits in silence, slowly rolling her own fresh cigarette. Clucking her tongue in thought. Finally, she says, "No offense, I don't know, I'm *of course* no expert, but it doesn't sound *that* happy to me at all."

"Well, it *was*. In the beginning, it was. Before the fight. I guess you had to be there."

"You got laid and then had an argument with an ex-girlfriend. What's so happy about that?"

"Amelie isn't an ex-girlfriend. We didn't break up. She's dead. She killed herself. There's a big fucking difference."

She flinches. "Yeah, right, sure. I just mean it doesn't sound very happy. Apart from the fact you got laid. Again, I mean no offense, but she sounds like a BPD waif or something."

"What do you mean?"

"I mean your ex seems like she has a lot of problems herself. A little like this borderline personality girl my brother was dating. She got him fired from his job..." She trails off and waves the rest of the thought away with her cigarette smoke.

"She *did* have a lot of problems. *We both* had a lot of problems. A lot of them probably caused by me. But Amelie, she was special. Very special for me."

"Because you say she committed suicide?"

"No."

"Then, special how?"

"She had this special way of moving. Talking. A special way of saying my name. I know it sounds corny as hell, but when we were together there was *something*, something beyond all this." I wave my hands around the courtyard. "This daily, normal shit. It doesn't matter if we fought occasionally, or we hurt each other. When we were together, it was like déjà vu or something. As though I had already lived my life a thousand times over and each and every time was with her. I don't know what love is supposed to be like. I can't describe it. Maybe it's just a bullshit word on a Valentine's Day card. But whatever it was that we had, I think it was love or whatever name you want to give it."

"God, you're so right. That *is* fucking embarrassingly corny, Vincent." She shoves two fingers into her mouth, pretending to vomit. "You just completely crashed and burned in my perception of you. Sounded like I was talking to a teenage girl for a moment there. You *do* have a penis, right?"

"Shut up, you bitch." I laugh too loud to cover my embarrassment. "Men can't catch a break, can we? Women complain about toxic masculinity, but as soon as any guy shows some kind of deeper emotion than *Smash! Fuck! Kill!* women's snatches go from moist to desert dried."

"That's gross, Vin. I really fucking hate the word *moist.*" She shakes and shivers.

"Are you moist or desert dry right now, Beatrice? I need to know, dammit!"

"Oh God, I'm afraid to say. I'm extraordinarily dry. Like a very good gin." She laughs.

I laugh. It feels good. Great, actually.

But then she looks at me thoughtfully for a moment. "On a serious note though, do you think it's possible you loved her more than she might have loved you? What's it called? Like projection or something?"

"Projection?"

"Yeah, you know, when you project your own feelings onto other people. Like a mirror or something. What do they say? Put a girl on a pedestal and all that? I have that problem myself."

"Since when did you become Katherine?"

"I'm sorry. I didn't mean to upset you. It just seems that way. Anyway, I was just talking. I warned you; I say weird shit sometimes. Just ignore me if you want."

"You didn't upset me. You just don't know what you're talking about. You *need* therapy, you don't need to *give it out.*"

"You *are* upset."

"No, I'm not. Really."

"Are you sure? You look kind of pissed off to me. You're sweating." She goes to touch my forehead and I duck.

"I'm fucking not. I'm used to no one getting it. It wasn't a normal relationship. It was fucked-up, but I don't know, it was our fucked-up relationship. There was a baby, too."

"But there isn't now?"

"Yeah. She had an abortion. I don't really want to talk about it, though."

"Yeah, I can understand that. Speaking from experience. That kind of thing will bond people together for good or bad. Trauma bonding."

We hold each other's eyes for a long time. It doesn't feel awkward.

"There was this old homeless woman in my area when I was a kid and she always walked around town with this raggedy stuffed panda like it was her baby. I used to see her every day on the way to school or when I was coming home. Always with that fucking panda. Once she had it in this antique-looking, spooky Victorian pram with these large wheels. Real creepy stuff. I always wondered what happened to her real baby. Some people are happier pretending like that, I suppose. Someone should've helped her, though." Beatrice avoids eye contact.

I do, too. "She was happy doing what she wanted to."

"When I was in my first year of secondary school, in the winter, they found her frozen to death in the doorway of Woolworths. Still clasping onto that bear, or so I heard. I was just a kid at the time, but I should've done something." Beatrice pulls deeply on her cigarette, eyes glazed, focused on the eves of the roof.

"What could've you done?" I ask.

"I could've tried talking to her or something."

"I don't think that would've helped."

"You think?"

"Look, let's change the subject, huh, Beatrice?"

"Yeah, whatever." She pulls her lips into her mouth in agreement. Deep dimples appear in her cheeks. She looks beautiful in a lost kind of way.

"You have to tell me what your happy moment is now, so I can attempt to pull it apart at the seams as well. I bet it's pony rides and middle-class birthday parties and all that kind of shit, isn't it?"

"No, not at all. I don't think I even have a happy place. Don't think I've ever had one. That's why I was interested in yours, Vincent."

"Everyone in this place is depressed as fuck, but they've all got something to hold onto. You must have some kind of moment in your life that was, I don't know, *content* or something."

"Nope. *Niente. Nada.* Nothing." She shrugs.

"No wonder you're such a fucking grumpy bitch, huh?" I grin to let her know I'm attempting to alleviate the conversation once and for all.

It works.

"You're a bastard, aren't you?" She playfully blows smoke in my face.

"This moment isn't so bad, is it? Chatting with me? Could be considered a little happy. At least."

"You're a little full of yourself, aren't you?" She smiles.

I smile. We smoke for a little while, listening to two sparrows chirping back and forth to each other on the roof. Beatrice finally breaks the moment by complaining that it's become chilly and suggests we go in for lunch before all the jelly dessert is gone.

We stand and stretch. The air smells good, like autumn.

As we make our way across the courtyard, Beatrice pauses and takes my hand, tightly squeezing it. Her flesh is February cold. "I want to say thank you, Vincent."

"Why? I didn't do anything."

She smiles. The weary grin of a terminally ill patient. "Thank you for letting me talk about nothing at all. It was nice. It's been such a long time since I could just speak about the smaller things, you know? It makes me crazy to just talk about my emotions and how I'm feeling all the fucking time. It's fucking exhausting."

"Yeah, I know. No problem, Beatrice. I thought it was pretty nice, too."

"You made me feel almost normal for a little while. *Almost.*" She grins.

"Ditto, Beatrice." I breathe in the scent of *Chanel No. 5*. It's suddenly all around me. On the air. The palms of my hands. The collar of my robe. "Can you smell that?"

"Smell what? Did you fart, Vincent? You dirty bastard."

"No. Perfume. Can you smell perfume?"

"Perfume? Nope, just our bad body odor and that putrid roast beef from the cafeteria."

I raise my palms to my face and breathe in deeply. All I can smell is the too-sweet scent of tobacco and sweat. Amelie's perfume is gone.

Beatrice observes me with a frown. "Vincent, you *can* get better, you know?"

"People keep telling me that. Sometimes I'm not sure I even want to get better."

"What a peculiar thing to say, no? Don't you want to get out of this fucking madhouse?"

"It's hardly a madhouse, but no, I don't think so. There's nothing left outside of this place for me. I don't want to be outside with the crowds and their social media bullshit and lies and all that other stuff. All I have left is what's up here," I say, tapping at my temple with a straight finger and cocked thumb like it's a pistol pressed to my head. For a few seconds, I think about all the famous people who killed themselves by gunshot. Ernest Hemingway in his kitchen one morning. Kurt Cobain above his garage. Richard Brautigan on his ranch. Hunter S. Thompson. All my heroes have committed suicide. I wonder why for me it's always been death by hanging. Guilt? Or maybe guns are just nearly impossible to get in the U.K..

The perfume comes back in waves like a migraine. I can taste it. I stagger on the concrete and brace myself with my fingers clenched into my kneecaps. Hunched over, breathing deeply, in the throes of something like a heart attack. The cobblestone underneath my feet blur and shimmer like water.

I'm in the warm water of a bath. Mine and Amelie's legs entwine around each other. The sounds of slow-moving liquid. Water caressing water—fingers softly pressing on ivory piano keys. Moist skin in the golden heat of candlelight. She's murmuring for me to kiss her, hold her. The taste of her skin and her perfume in my mouth. She always loved fucking in the bath. In water.

Not bath water. It's rainwater. I'm walking down a desolate night street in heavy rain. Soaked through. Staggering in the dark. This is where we ended. This is where Amelie died.

"You can't stay in this place forever, Vincent. You need to wake up and go home," Beatrice sighs loudly. She's standing on the drenched street next to me. Her hand on my shoulder.

"What do you mean?" I croak, coming out of the haze. The real purgatory of memory.

"Snap out of it! You're not really sick. You're still fast asleep. Still dreaming. Wake up, Vincent. Wake up and smell the coffee. Wake up and smell the fucking coffee! Wake the fuck up and smell the fucking coffee! Smell the fucking coffee, Vincent!" She's screaming at the top of her lungs. My heart feels as though it's decomposing in my chest. I can't breathe.

Idiot faces appear at grimy windows, gawking slack-jawed at Beatrice as two of the support staff, maybe Michael and Greg, march over and attempt to quieten her down. All palms and faux-caring expressions. I stumble to the side and watch as everything plays out. An out-of-body experience. A bystander pathetically observing. My heartbeat slows to a murmur. Sucking air through a pinprick down into my palsied body. Sick. Lovesick. Drug addict sick. My arms clamped to my chest now, not because of the pain, but because I don't know what else to do with my hands, and if I do something, I'm afraid I'll hurt someone. Hurt myself.

Finally, they pull Beatrice by the arms, squirming back towards her room, and she glances back at me over her shoulder as they take her away. Her blue eyes wide, on a bad trip. Full of a damp sadness. She shouts at me one more time to wake up. I'm still dreaming. Then she's gone and the courtyard is desolate. Silent as though Beatrice had never been here at all.

The scent of Amelie is all around me. In the air. She is the only season there will ever be. That ever was.

I stumble back to my room and collapse on my bed, bury my face in the starched hospital pillow. Suddenly drowning in black. Hyperventilating.

I feel empty.

I am a bathtub with the plug pulled.

I am the plug hole.

I am the darkness that travels down into darker darkness.

I am the gray, bitter rainfall.

I am the slammed door.

I am the knot in the noose.

I am the blackest black hole.

One word repeated over and over in my skull.

The only word.

Projection.

SEVEN

Towards the end of lunch, I compose myself enough to enter the cafeteria. Everyone stops eating to gawk at me.

I eyeball them all back, one by one until they return to spooning crap into their gaping, agony-shaped mouths.

Beatrice isn't amongst them. Perhaps, after her outburst, she feels embarrassed and is eating alone in her room. Or maybe they've just given her so many sedatives, she's out for the count. I wanted to ask her what she meant by me needing to wake up and smell the coffee. Why did she say that? I've heard it before but don't know where it's from. Did I do or say something to upset her?

Disappointed, I glance around the few crowded tables, searching for a place I can sit on my own. Some people still glance apprehensively at me for some reason. But most don't. Most of these people I know well. Some I don't.

There's the kid, Lewis, a bald 18-year-old who can't stop cutting himself. Maeve, a very pretty 25-year-old suffering from bipolar disorder and addiction. Martha, in her fifties, a delusional schizophrenic. Johnathan, a 36-year-old depressive schizophrenic. Malik or Farad or George or Alex, an Iranian guy who refuses to introduce himself to anyone and gives out fake names. He's in his late forties, I think. I don't know the exact diagnosis for him. He thinks he was a spy and had to assassinate people for the government. There's the ex-lawyer, Jeanette. She's in her early fifties and a schizophrenic who thinks people are trying to murder her. I often wonder if maybe she isn't sick at all. She could've written one hell of a crime novel. Haley, late forties but looks much older, borderline personality disorder. Jim, early forties, he's a chronic obsessive compulsive and carries a plastic spray bottle full of water everywhere to clean surfaces. He freaks out if you touch him. Sometimes I touch him on purpose just to watch him freak out. Crazy-haired Norman looks like the doc from *Back to the Future*, also in his forties with bipolar disorder.

Most of them are past their second stay at the clinic and their second helping of jelly dessert. They don't talk too much, and the overriding atmosphere is that of a prison canteen.

In all the movies and all the books, they make you believe that people in these kinds of places make friends, lasting relationships that change everyone's lives for the better. Clean, bright wards, and corridors of lovable, affable, kooky characters only momentarily damaged but easily fixed by the time the credits roll or the last page is turned. The hero's journey to sanity and health and normalcy. It's absolute bullshit. No one here wants to make friends. There are no late-night poker games, no fashion shows or any of that stupid Hollywood crap. Everyone in this place just wants to be left the fuck alone and none of these people will ever be easily fixed. If at all.

We are the twisted, rusted refuse washed ashore from human shipwrecks and natural disasters. Every single one of us has let the demons in through the back door and now we have to party with them. Demons love to party. They snort railway lines of coke and won't be leaving for a long, long time. A house party in Hell and it's all in our heads. *Party, motherfucker! Dance!*

I spot a vacant seat at the end of the table nearest the window and queue up with my tray for the penitentiary-style cuisine. Trying to remember what day of the week it is. *Wednesday? Thursday? Sunday?* Like many other things, I've been here too long and don't know anymore. Don't care. It's not like it really matters. There are no days in Limbo. A day is just a different name for something that is exactly the same. It's just 24 hours repeated. Sped up. Slowed down. Paused. Rewound. Fast-forwarded. A VHS played until static lines the edges of the image. Black and gray. Gray and black. The color of an ultrasound scan. Of things burnt. Of ash. That early morning broadcasting picture of a grinning little girl playing noughts and crosses with a clown doll.

The panpipe version of "Can't Help Falling in Love" plays in the background again. Vertigo hits like a blue door slammed shut in my face. Dizzy. I stagger and grab hold of the tray-return trolley for balance and glare at Davina, the petite, birdlike nurse serving the food like everything is all her fault. She smiles with ivory teeth, waving me forward. Dinner is over-boiled baby potatoes, limp broccoli and soggy roast beef with gravy served in a tinfoil tray like a manic-depressant's TV dinner.

Dessert is always the same powdery strawberry jelly in the same small paper cups.

The bitter scent of the food mixed with the cloying stench of sweat, chlorine, and disinfectant always makes me gag. The one thing I've never gotten used to. The stink of mental illness in confined spaces. If someone doesn't have the energy to keep on living, good luck getting them to wash properly.

I don't feel hungry at all. I don't want to eat anything. Can't eat anything, but I have to, so they'll leave me alone. Eating less means I can gain a trance-like state easier. Improving my meditation. My concentration. Memories become much more vivid, more controllable. More alive. Eating their food and taking their meds makes me groggy, hungover. Things and people pass me by so quickly, they grow into blinding strobes of light, erratically dancing in my periphery. Dazed. Confused. Concentration snapping like dried-out rubber bands.

No focus.

Amelie fades to a pale whisper of cigarette smoke flashing through a telescope peered through at the wrong end. That jumbled kaleidoscope of dull memories and mistakes that lead to death. That lead to here.

All roads lead here.

Limbo.

The clinic.

The end of the line.

The End.

I seat myself at the table, staring down at the food with sandpaper eyes. The clotted, shit-colored gravy catching at the smoggy light of day and seeping into everything. I gag again but attempt to relax my gourd with the calming thought of shoving two tobacco-stained fingers down my throat to vomit in the toilet later. Hurrying there when I see the support staff at their most preoccupied. Maybe trying to convince the ex-lawyer Jeanette that no one has poisoned her jelly. Or explaining to the Iranian again that he never killed a Soviet agent and chopped him into little pieces to be spread down the M25 motorway. They're just delusions. Long shadows in a midday sun. Memories that aren't memories at all. Wake up and smell the fucking coffee.

It's an act. I'm eating their food and taking their pills strictly for show. For the ballpoint pen checkmarks next to my name on a government-issued clipboard. I've been regurgitating it as much as possible, but it's difficult. I have to get the amount right. Not too much or they'll notice my weight loss. Just enough to get the meds out of my system so I'll be able to think straight.

I poke at my dinner with a plastic fork with dull tines. Tell myself I'm gaming the system. But I know I'm only winning a hand of poker while slowly bleeding out at the game table. Treading water with crocodiles. Swimming against a current. Starting a fire in a rainstorm. My brain is an hourglass shattered on concrete. Death is inevitable. I am surfing a tsunami. Shooting up with a bad dose. Playing Russian roulette with a sawn-off shotgun. Suicide feels like an old friend that I haven't seen in a long time but can't wait to meet.

My love is dead.

Gone.

All I have are memories. *Memento mori.* Recollections making me sick, *they* say. *They* have college and university degrees perfectly framed on office walls, but they don't know Amelie. They don't know about loss. They don't even know what love *is.* They don't know it's the love that injures and traumatizes that we all hold onto the tightest, like a tiger at the end of a short rope.

Shared trauma is love.

Love is shared trauma.

Love scars. Love disables. Love deforms. Love cripples.

Love is fentanyl. Love is Heroin. Love is Crack. Love is the finest Scotch.

We're all broken-down addicts, drowning in our cravings. Withdrawals. Scratching and muttering to ourselves. Tearing ourselves into pieces. Confetti of bone and blood.

Love.

There are no recoveries here. No anonymous meetings in stuffy church halls or community centers. No twelve steps. No sobriety coins. No medals. No chips. Only overdoses in lonely motel rooms. Discover me when I'm bloated purple and crawling with blowflies. I loved too much. Too hard.

Amelie, I love you. I need you. I killed you. You wrecked me and only you can fix me.

A fix for me.

Good evening, everyone, my name is Vincent and I'm an addict…

Yes, the therapists and doctors think I'm sick. *They're* sick. They assume their education protects them from madness. Shields them. Sanity is a frayed lace on a shit-caked shoe. Snapping when you least suspect it. I know all this; therefore, I'm not sick. I'm not ill. I killed the woman I love. I am guilty. I am beyond depressed. I'm full of dirty rainwater. I am out of gas and idling at a cliff edge. But I'm not sick.

I am *not* sick.

Perhaps, *that* is what Beatrice meant. What she was trying to tell me. To realize I'm not sick. I am not mentally ill. I'm not crazy.

Who is crazy? Someone for trying to die or them for forcing someone to live?

Swallow down these handfuls of pills and you'll feel all better.

Drag yourself shuffling through these echo-loop days.

Let's discuss your shitty childhood and your distant relationships. About being bullied at school. How no one ever liked you.

Let's discuss the job you hate and how you're unfulfilled. Unsatisfied.

Let's talk about your boss and how he doesn't respect you.

Let's discuss the woman you love who walked away and left you for fucking dead.

Let's blame it on everyone and everything else but yourself and your own sins.

Let's get it all off your chest and you'll be right as rain in no time.

Here, take these pills and go to sleep. Sleep a lot. Sleep as much as possible. Watch television. Go shopping. Tell everyone bullshit on social media. Learn to hate. Project. Listen to the news. Stay a child for as long as possible. Dream. Fantasize.

Amelie is still dead. Cremated, ashes scattered off the boardwalk. I wasn't even invited to the fucking funeral. If I got over it easily, moved on, fucked around with girls from bars, nightclubs, and dating websites, would I then be considered a sane, healthy person? I think it's another one of life's bullshit catch-22s. The crazy people walk the streets, and the sanest people are all locked up in places like this.

Love is madness.

Each time you fall in love, you lose a piece of yourself. Something is given away. Or stolen. Or ripped from you. I'm in love with a ghost.

Amelie.

My love is dead.

"Yep, this is the same grub as yesterday, innit, mate? I just told them that, but they didn't even give a shit, yeah. I told them, 'Hey, oi, this is the same food as yesterday, yeah.' That's exactly what I said to them when I went to get my lunch just now, yeah. They don't even bat an eyelid, mate. Don't care. Don't give a shit. What *is* the National fucking Health Service coming to? I'd sure like to know. Yep, I surely would, mate, yeah."

I glance up from my foil tray and flinch. It's the guy who accidentally locked himself in the courtyard—Mark. He looks like the Cabbage Patch doll my sister had. His small, crowded face could be 18 or 84. Blue eyes, red-lined and tearfully dazed. Wearing a torn, navy body-warmer over a stained vest and Bermuda shorts. Something wrong with his closely shaved head. It's too large for his short beanbag body. His brain is swelling through his cranium. It's dripping out through his nose and ears, he often tells people who don't ask him. An only slightly prettier version of the Elephant Man. I don't know why he's in the clinic or why his nostrils are constantly stuffed with bloodstained tissues. I don't want to know his diagnosis because I just don't care. I have my own problems, obviously.

He picks dried blood from his rubbery upper lip and drops flakes of it onto the sticky tabletop next to his tray. I cringe. His fingernails are caked in clotted claret, and he stinks like an underground carpark. I lower my head again, staring down into the food. Roast beef now well-past soggy. Barely edible. Holding my breath. I don't want to be a prick. Mark's an okay guy, I guess. I just don't want to get stuck listening to him rattle on. Or look at his face and head. It's too sad.

I want to be left alone.

"I tried to call my dad this morning from that green pay phone in the common room, but he wasn't home, yeah. He's got a new wife now, hasn't he? She's the one I spoke to. *Her.* The bitch! I should've pushed her off a cliff, right? Like you did, Captain Save-A-Hoe?"

"What did you just say to me?"

He doesn't even hear me, jabbering on. "She told me my dad was at work and then put me on hold for hours. Lying, lying, lying bitch! She's a complete fucking lying bitch! Excuse my

French. Thinks she's hot shit because she was an extra in a couple of movies. *Mulholland Drive*, you seen it?

"No, I haven't."

"Too triggering for you, yeah? My real mum died in a car accident. It was really, really, really sad. I don't think I've ever cried that much. I still miss her every day. My *real* mum, I mean. Anyway, I wanted to ask my dad if he was going to come visit me, yeah? I haven't seen him in like a month, I think. I'm not sure though. I could really use some spending money, yeah?" He pauses to squeeze an overripe yellow head on his chin, wiping the pus on the underside of the table, and then continues his narrative with renewed enthusiasm. "I really don't like his new wife *at all,* mate. She's a complete fucking cunt. Excuse my French. She doesn't like me, but you know what? I don't care. I don't. I don't fucking care, yeah. Not one fucking iota, mate. She's the reason I'm in this fucking place. She tricked my dad into putting me in here. She's got him wrapped around her little finger. Fucking pisses me off, yeah. And this, this is the same grub as yesterday. I'm sick of roast fucking beef, I could cut the tongue right out of my head. Jump right off a cliff. I need more change for the payphone. Could you lend me 20 pence or a quid or something, mate? 50 pence?"

"No, sorry, Mark," I say, staring at a droplet of gravy soaking into the sleeve of my robe.

I could tell him that the pay phone in the common room hasn't worked since before I got here. It used to have an A4 sheet of paper saying, **OUT OF ORDER** taped to it, but someone ripped it up and scattered it around like bird shit. I could tell him he's always muttering down a dead line. But I don't. What would be the point? I'm sure he already knows the line is dead and probably prefers it that way. Like the story Beatrice told. The old woman with the stuffed panda. I clear my throat at the thought. Slowly chewing my roast beef and avoiding Mark's darting, jaundiced, reaching eye contact.

The old man people call Bertie, who years ago had a mental breakdown after his wife cheated on him with the next-door neighbor, and who spends his time stumbling around the clinic in circles, scrounging cigarettes and shouting about the betrayal, staggers over to our table, shoving a gnarled claw underneath my nose. "Dave! Dave, a cigarette? Can I have a cigarette? Cigarette, please."

The first few weeks at the clinic, I must have given him a whole carton of cigarettes and told him a thousand times my name wasn't Dave. I've learnt to ignore him. These days, I'm running low on cigarettes. Running low on patience. Running low on just about everything.

Mark drones on like a wasp trapped underneath a glass tumbler. Bertie keeps his dirty palm open in front of my face like a plucked dead bird. Of all the patients in the clinic, I always find Bertie's presence the most disquieting. It's as though I'm gazing into the limpid eyes of an older version of myself. What I may become if I live that long. I don't want *that*. I am not him. I'm not the same as these people. I want to scream. Slam my tray into their hopeless faces, but I don't. That would only make things worse for me. I'd be moved again. Tranquilized like a zoo animal. Drugged up. A shuffling coma case like Bertie. Put under constant observation.

I close my eyes. Tune out. "Can't Help Falling in Love" drifts from the speakers, growing in tempo until the crescendo bursts, shooting out into long, bright lines twisting through a pitch black. Like iridescent fireworks watched by a child on a father's shoulders one November night. A Guy Fawkes mannequin burning on the bonfire. The Guy's mask melts away, and I see it's myself burning. Drowning in flames.

I stumble away through the darkness, dragged along to a door cast in the gloomy yellow of a streetlamp.

It's raining.

I'm full of rainwater and trembling. Sweating. Drenched in wet fear. Burning up in a fever of hopelessness.

The door is heavy wood. Painted a shade of dark blue I will always think of as police siren blue. End of the line blue. The door has a brass knocker shaped like an urn. Ashes to ashes. Dust to dust. Smooth and worn out in places. I watch a hand hesitating, twitching like a dying spider above the knocker for a long time before the fingertips fumble at the latch and finally use it. The other hand grasps a plastic convenience store bag. A small tub of vanilla ice cream, packets of crisps and some boxes of chocolates inside. The ice cream and chocolates have melted long ago. The hands are my own.

The day is August 4th. A Thursday. A day branded into the core of myself—a gangrenous tattoo. A day of dying. Of murder. Things rot. Things fall apart. The center cannot hold.

The day that might've been the beginning of the end for Amelie and me.

The day of the abortion.

The end.

It's a long time before the door creaks open. The same taint of blue flooding down the hallway and out into the night from a television set in a cramped living room, around the silhouette of a shadow person. Amelie's flat mate. Another American girl named Hanna. Moonfaced, bookish, overweight, sexless Hanna. A medical student from Michigan studying for a doctorate at one of the universities here in the city. She doesn't like me and lets me know it every time I come around to the small, ground-floor apartment. Swiveling her harsh ebony eyes in my direction and staring as though I'm a half-dead insect scurrying across a cracked wall, dragging its guts along behind it. She's older, more experienced than Amelie, and thinks I'm a complete piece of shit. She's right. Especially today. I am the worst kind of shit.

"Yuck, you smell like you've been drinking all day." She wrinkles her mousy nose in disgust. Glancing me up and down—ice-cold.

"That your medical diagnosis, is it?"

"Oh, you don't even wanna know what my medical diagnosis would be for you, buddy. I can't believe you spent today, of all days, drinking."

"No, not *all* day, Hanna. Just one or two on the way here. I was thirsty," I mumble, feeling like a kid in front of a disappointed parent. A jagged pain ripping through my guts, reminding me why I'm here. I'm here because Amelie aborted my child today. How many weeks along was she? 10 seconds, 10 weeks, 10 months. It doesn't matter. A life is a life is a life. A heartbeat is a heartbeat is a heartbeat is a heartbeat. I am a selfish murderer and from this day forth, the blue door to Hell awaits me, standing ajar. Creaking open, wider, wider.

"You should've been there, Vincent." Hanna clucks her tongue, sighs dramatically. Rolling her eyes.

If I wasn't on the verge of tears again, I'd knock the spiteful bitch on her arse. "I know. I had to…work," I mumble. Fucking pathetic.

"Work? That's the worst excuse I've ever heard, Vincent. *I* went with her in the end."

In the end.

"Thank you," I say, eager to get the conversation over with. I've relived this many times. We've already exchanged these exact words over and over again. I just want to see Amelie. Need to see Amelie.

"It's all right. I wanted to go with her. She couldn't go on her own, could she?" She places her hands on her hips. A warped Dali painting of a pair of scissors.

"She told me she wanted to." I attempt to push past her, but she blocks my way with a spiteful arm.

"And you believed her?" She clucks her tongue again.

I fumble with the carrier bag. Scratching at my neck. Blinking stupidly like I'm taking Polaroids with my itchy eyes. "Please, just let me see her. I've been trying to call her all day. Her phone's switched off again," I recite the script verbatim of what happened that day.

"Yeah, alright, fine. She's resting in her room. You *should* go in. She *needs* you now. Though I don't know why. Better late than never, I guess." She sinks back into the blue haze and canned laughter of the television, leaving the door open for me. I step inside and close it, not onto a London street but onto the cafeteria in the clinic. Mark stares, goggled-eyed. He waves at me, awed and bewildered. Bertie is shouting something. His scraggly mouth opening and closing. He seems to be calling me back. I can't hear a word he's saying. I close the door. They cease to exist.

They were never real.

I was never real.

Amelie's bedroom is joined onto the hallway to the left. Her door slightly ajar, spilling out warm light from the reading lamp next to her bed.

I wipe at my face with my knuckles and check my reflection in a hallway mirror. Eyes still bloodshot and swollen from hours of standing slumped behind the garages across the street with my face in my hands. I cried for many reasons that day. All of them selfish.

I push open Amelie's door wider, it stone-cold underneath my palm. The hinges creak softly. The scent of her room, perfume, Chanel No. 5, and a mixture of gray ocean spray washes over me in a damp backdraft. She's curled into a ball on the peach-colored bedsheets, face buried in a pillow. Blonde hair spread infinitely over the fabric. She looks small and fragile. Childlike. It's a kick to the guts. I grab at the frame of the doorway for balance. Breathless.

Amelie reaches out for me. Repeating my name in a voice whispered desperately like a prayer in the night.

In her room like this, it feels as though we have lived this trauma over and over. And in my head, we have.

I have.

I'm observing this scene from the corner of the room, whilst also participating in it. An out-of-body experience. A soul floating above the convulsing body of a flat-lining trauma patient. The ghost haunting its own past.

I drop the carrier bag onto the carpet. A blood-splashed orange rolls across the floor. Letting Amelie pull me onto the bed next to her. She surprises me with a flurry of kisses. Lips and cheeks tasting of seawater. Her skin fever-hot. Wet stains— raindrops scattered over the linen sheets and pillows. Not moist stains of love this time, but ones of a much deeper hurt. That's what I have done to this woman.

I am a piece of shit.

There is a jagged scar inside her now that will fester until the day she dies. That's the wound I've inflicted on her. This woman I love. She wanted a baby, I did not. I told her I wouldn't be a father to that child. Didn't want to be involved. Blamed her for lying about being on birth control. Allowed her mother to badger her into the procedure by long distance telephone call. I stood by, saying nothing. A mute devil's advocate. A speechless and cowardly piece of shit. Letting the mother who she already hated apply all of the unpleasant pressure. Reassuring myself that maybe the kid wasn't even mine. All those times we fought, and the nights she disappeared. Her phone switched off. She called me a paranoid freak. I called her a lying bitch. All the times we threw each other away and then caught each other as we fell. Antidotes for insecurities. Toxic medication for shared trauma. Deep down, in my heart, I always knew the baby was mine. The child. My child. Felt it at the very bottom of my gut. My being. My soul. A knowing.

In my room, in the clinic, I try to calculate how old the baby would be now. If it had lived. If I'd been a better man. I lose count of the months, the years, and become confused.

Disappearing down the rabbit hole of *what if* and *but*. I contemplate parallel universes where the child lives and will start its own family tree, the roots stretching centuries into the future.

When you commit murder, you don't just kill a single person. You destroy a whole fragment of the future. You wipe out hundreds of people and everything that could've been.

Amelie lifts her pillow to reveal the print-out of the last ultrasound scan she had taken a week before. She will show it to me many times. I still see it whenever I close my eyes. Burnt into my eyelids. She holds it in her trembling hands, delicately placing it to her lips to kiss it. My eyes snag on the name she's written in ballpoint pen next to the black dot that would have been her child. Our child. My child.

Now, we're only the parents of sin. Mother and father to a bastard named guilt.

Over the remnants of what little is left of our relationship. The ultrasound will be used as a weapon. Pulled from Amelie's handbag and brandished in my face like a long-bladed knife every time we argue.

She never got over it.

I can never get over her.

August 4th.

I lost her that day.

Lost myself.

Stumbling around town, drunk with all my selfish relief as she lay herself down on a hospital cot, stepping up to the gallows, some doctor in an executioner's hood. If she searched for my face in the crowd, I know she never saw it there. That was the reason I forgave her betrayals. I had committed the biggest betrayal of all.

For here and now, this moment, this memory, I take her in my arms, her hair brittle straw underneath my fingertips, her tears soaking into my clothes, and I hold her tightly, trembling into something resembling sleep.

On her bedside table is an empty white mug with a coffee stain at the bottom. The mug says ***happy dayz*** in childish blue script. There's a crack on the lip. I stay awake as Amelie sleeps and I stare at the mug.

After a minute or an hour, I fall unconscious too. I dream. It is a dream within a dream. Amelie is dead and gone. There's only the lightness and darkness of passing time.

Limbo. Lime green and burnt orange.

Repeat. Recycle. Birth. Death. Rebirth. Death. Limbo. Breakfast. Pills. Classes. Therapy. Lunch. Pills. Therapy. Visitations. Dinner. Pills. Tea and toast. Bed. Lights out. Breakfast. Pills. Classes. Therapy. Lunch. Pills. Therapy. Visitations. Dinner. Pills. Tea and toast. Bed. Lights out. Breakfast. Pills. Classes. Therapy. Lunch. Pills. Therapy. Visitations. Dinner. Pills. Tea and toast. Bed. Lights out.

Lights out.

The end.

Rebirth.

I am in Purgatory.

I am in a mental hospital now.

They say I am in crisis.

I can see my parents.

Mother. Father.

EIGHT

I am eight years old again.

My mother and father bring me to a dim room where my brain is checked to see if it's broken. The room is gray like the television screen when it can't find a channel. A dry stink of dust floating in the air.

A large, black leather chair looming in the middle of the tile—a deformed dead pig. On shelves scattered around the room, many plastic dolls stare down at me. Naked, pink dolls with all their hair hacked off. Only small blonde and brown sprouts remain on the little, hole-speckled skulls. Hats like helmets of wire and glittering tinfoil pinned in their scalps with glinting pins. The dolls' eyes watch me. Dead lips smiling small, dead smiles. Inside my stomach, it's the lukewarm rainwater collected in a flowerpot after a storm in the backyard. I cut a worm in half with a plastic beach shovel and wonder if God will send me to Hell for it.

My mother's hand is hot, squeezing mine as she leads me up to the monster-like chair. I don't like the chair. It's the chair they tie the bad guys in and fry their brains like rotten eggs. I'm a bad guy.

An overweight woman with hair the color of dead leaves thumps through the doorway. She is wearing a mad scientist's white coat, and square glasses with thick lenses that make her eyes too big and too wet. She shakes my hand lightly. Her fingers are very cold. The woman points at the dolls and their little, painful hats with a silver pen like the straight razor my father uses to shave. I keep looking at my mother's face. She's very young here. Her eyes sparkle like broken bottles in sunlight, her lips are stretched very thinly across her jaw. She tickles my hair. I yawn. Suddenly sleepy. Drugged. But I can't sleep. My mouth is very dry as though I'm thirsty, but I'm not. I drank orange squash a little while before, and now I need to go pee-pee.

My father is in the waiting room, reading old copies of *Yacht Owner Supplement*. He has never owned a yacht and has never wanted one, could never dream of affording one, but he reads it while they check my brain. I don't know why, and neither does he. When I gaze out through the doorway into the waiting room, searching for Amelie, she isn't there. All I can see are the bottoms of my father's legs draped in blue denim and his tan shoes. The shoes jump and dance strangely on the green carpet to music I can't hear. I don't want to hear that music.

The woman with the large eyes bubbling behind the windowpane lenses slides out a long, gray needle from a drawer. She pretends to gently scratch at a doll's head with it. The doll stares at me with dead eyes. The eyes are deep brown. The color of Amelie's. The woman nods and nods as she demonstrates something I don't understand. I nod too so no one will be disappointed in me. They all think my brain is broken because I tied the belt around my neck and tried to hang myself. They wanted to know why I did that, but I didn't know why. It was just a feeling inside me. Something like an empty shoebox in my stomach.

I don't like this place. I want to go home. I want to be with Amelie, but I haven't met her yet. She's four and living in Atlantic City with her mother. Maybe her father hasn't drunk himself to death yet, maybe he's still there, too.

My mother pushes me into the cold arms of the chair by gently resting her palms on my chest. I feel safe when her fingers weigh down on me. I lie down. I'm gazing at the ceiling, the icy cushioning of the leather on my back, my T-shirt and sweater ridden up a little.

I wish my mother would leave her hand on my chest. Feeling my heartbeat underneath her palm, but she pulls it away and rests it in her lap with her other hand. Holding hands with herself. A tissue choked in her grip. Sitting the way that she used to in church.

We don't go to church anymore.

The woman in the white coat clicks on a light hanging over the chair on a long, metal neck that swings in different directions. It looks like an alien on a flying saucer from a movie we watched at my grandmother's house before she died. The light's very bright. It shines through my eyelids, making colorful pictures of orange lines and red zigzags. Like the magic tube you put to your eye and move around and there are mirrors and shapes and stuff inside it. I can never say what that thing is called. *Collide-a-skops?*

The woman in the white coat sighs. Her breath smells of milky coffee. I'm not allowed to drink coffee. It's not for children. Not allowed in the clinic either. She switches on a gray machine beside her cluttered desk. The machine hums. She places something like a helmet on my head, similar to the ones the dolls have, but mine is bigger. This is the part where they'll fry my brain because I'm a bad guy. I did something bad and now I'm here. Amelie wanted the baby. I was relieved when she had the abortion.

A porcelain cow stands on a pile of papers on the desk. It has a tiny gold bell tied around its neck with a bright red ribbon like the belt I tried to hang myself with. Or the drawstring cord from a pair of baggy joggers—Amelie used to wear around my apartment—I'll drunkenly knot into a noose and tie to the top of the bathroom door. My future is my past. My life is an infinite loop.

My mother sits in front of me, and the woman asks her to move out of the way, and my mother does. She drops her balled-up tissue onto the shiny floor. It's a snowball I made last winter for a moment, but then it's just tissue paper again and my mother picks it up, quickly pushing it into her handbag.

The machine whirrs and clicks, annoyed with my brain. The bug-eyed woman tells me to relax. She tells me the machine is connected to my special helmet. The special helmet sends messages to my brain using the needles and then, if my brain is working okay or not, it will send messages back to the machine. "Just like that," she says. *Just like that.* I'm a very brave astronaut, the woman says. I nod and try to smile, but I want to cry. I think being an astronaut must be very lonely. Lost in all that nothingness. Far away from everything and everyone in complete darkness. I live in that place.

I need to go to the toilet. I don't want to piss my pants again.

My mother and father thought that my brain wasn't working properly since they found the belt around my neck and kept screaming and crying at me. Shaking me. Asking me what was wrong with me. Did I want to die? Or maybe, they thought I was sick since blood came out of my ear and nose and I closed my eyes tight, let myself fall from that swing onto my face, into the small stones and little pieces of wood in the park across from our house. It was hot that day. My mother carried me home in her arms like a baby.

There's sometimes scribbled, crumpled, black paper inside my head that makes my body feel empty. Hollow. I don't ever tell my parents this. I can't explain it with the words I know. I want to tell them I'm not the astronaut. I am the darkness floating in outer space.

The special hat is placed more firmly on my head like a crown. Not an astronaut or space itself. I am a king now. King Arthur. The King of Hearts. The Suicide King. Or maybe, I am like Jesus. The crown Jesus wears in church looks painful. It's stabbing his head and blood comes out. I'm not Jesus. Jesus was a good guy. He died for my sins. I'm the bad guy. I'm going to fry and go to Hell.

The robot woman scratches and stabs at my skull with the long knitting needle. She wants to get inside there. I gaze at Amelie sitting next to the monitor and Amelie gazes at me. I try to be strong, act like a grown-up. Tell her I love her and I'm sorry for being a bad boy. She screws up her face and her lips make wavy, sad lines. I look down at my shoes because I don't want to cry. My shoes are special. They're called Hi-Tec. I can run faster and jump higher when I wear them. My grandmother bought them for me. She used to take me to school because my mother and father were working early in the mornings. Sometimes, she let me stay home with her and took me shopping. I didn't like the indoor parking garage at the supermarket. It smelled old and damp like sadness. My grandmother said many people had killed themselves there. Gassed themselves in their cars or hung themselves from the roof. When we were walking back to her small green car with the bags of food, I felt those dead people place their hands on my shoulders. Saw them out of the corner of my eye. They wanted to be friends with me, but they scared me.

The gray machine beside the leather bed-chair jumps into life and starts writing something on long pieces of white paper that tumble from its slit-mouth.

I lay watching the dolls, listening to the machine scribbling, and wondering what will happen if my brain turns out to be no good. Busted. Broken. Will I be made to go and live somewhere else, far away from my mother and father? A boarding school for bad kids or the hospital on the hill where older kids at school say the crazy people live. I don't want to be taken away.

I reach out for Amelie's hand but she's not there anymore. It's my mother's hand. She squeezes my fingers, almost painfully, looking at me for a long time and smiling but the smile is strange. It's not really a smile. It only goes up halfway and then it stops and falls back down into those sad, wavy lines again. I'm dying and my mother knows I am already dead, but she's holding it as a secret somewhere inside her. I know, I am a shadow you see out of the corner of your eye. One of the dead people in the supermarket parking garage.

My stomach is very tight and small. I want to go pee-pee real bad, it burns. My chest feels cold and like a big rock underneath my *Teenage Mutant Ninja Turtles* sweater. I'm very frightened.

The dolls stare and stare and don't stop. My mother squeezes and squeezes my hand and my father reads and reads the magazine in the waiting room.

The machine finally becomes tired and stops writing down the suicide letters from my brain. It goes to sleep, humming to itself. The monster in the white coat straightens her long brown skirt, and tears the long message from the mouth of the machine. Holding it in her big claw hands and reading it carefully like it's my spelling test and I've done badly again. Her large eyes swing back and forth, back and forth, like the machinery stuff in my grandfather's large clock. She licks her lips, takes it over to her desk and sits down with it. Making circles with a pencil that has a dirty pink eraser on top.

I watch my mother watching the woman as she scribbles and circles on Amelie's letter. When she's finished, she puts down the pencil and leaves the room. I look at my mother to see what her face is saying. Does she understand what's going on here? Does she know the meaning? The mystery of this old lady in the white coat, and the pencil scribbling. But her eyes are red, and she looks very tired, like she's finished her night shift. How she looks when she cried a lot and became exhausted from too much sadness and had to go live in a clinic for a while after Grandma's heart broke and she died. I remember visiting my mother in that place with my sister and brother. There were brown, dying roses and people sitting around, doing nothing but smoking cigarette after cigarette. Every person in that place seemed to be waiting for something to happen but they didn't know what it was they were supposed to be waiting for.

Frankenstein in the white coat returns and takes my mother outside to talk away from me. I only hear whispers floating into the room like my father's cigarette smoke when he's working in the garage at home.

After a little while, my mother returns, lifts me up and carries me out to the car park. I want to walk on my own. I don't want to be like a baby. She's holding me too tight.

My father is sitting in the front seat of his white car, waiting. He's smoking a cigarette and I like the scent as the blue smoke drifts out on the cool air from the open window towards me.

In the car, he leans over, wraps me up in the seatbelt and asks if I would like some comics or sweets or something. I say yes, but I need to go pee-pee. My father nods and smiles, but I know he didn't hear me at all.

The car starts down the street. My mother's crying again and my father has one hand on her leg. After a while, as the piss bursts free, running down my leg, puddling onto the seats, he takes his hand away from her, switches on the radio and just keeps on driving.

NINE

They sit hunched awkwardly together in the bitter November gray of the courtyard.

My parents.

Waiting for me.

I stand, watching them. My mother smoking cigarette after cigarette, head hung low. Poor woman probably thought she'd seen the back of this building years ago, but she's returned time and time again to see her children within the same walls. Visitations of the blood. Each of her offspring broken in different ways. These days, not here for herself, or her eldest son, nor her youngest daughter. It's for me, the youngest son.

There's no escaping this place, Mum. It's Limbo. An infinite loop. Once you've stepped foot here, into the void, it sticks to you. Soaking into the fabric of your clothes like droplets of rain. The pores of your skin. The hair follicles on your scalp. The genetic roots of our family tree are grown here. Metal illness a lingering stench you can never completely wash off. You get turned around in the corridors and lose your way. Haunted by all the things you can't remember nor forget. One foot in the past, one foot in the future, squatted down and shitting all over the present. Here in a skid row motel for hissed disquiet and the addicted walking wounded. *Here's your room key, you're booked in for eternity. Happy days. Enjoy your fucking stay.*

I observe my father as he scrutinizes his gold wristwatch three times, then solemnly peer around the courtyard, probably wishing he were sat at his desk, shooting the shit with normal people like the pretty receptionist, doodling on a notepad, or checking over his employees' clock cards. Or hell, doing anything else, anywhere else. I'd probably feel the same. *Who needs this kind of shit?*

I mirror his gesture, running my fingertips over the face of my wristwatch, the one gift from Amelie that remains unscathed. My eyes follow the second hand dancing around the face like the specter of a woman in a long, gray dress.

Occasionally, my father gazes down, nodding at his prematurely gnarled hands in his lap as if he's trying to decipher why everyone in his family is batshit crazy. Searching for faulty genetics in the lines etched across his palms and in between the swirls of his fingerprints.

I'm not crazy, Dad. I'm in that space between life and death. Of mourning. There's a difference. But once you're in Limbo, you're there. Marked. Labelled. Stuck. People only believe in what they want to think is real. Healthy or ill. Sane or insane. It doesn't really matter. People see what they want. Delusions for illusions. Only have to take a stroll down the local high street or scroll through social media to see the self-delusions on show. It's an epidemic. Fake people faking happiness. Faking personalities. Faking righteousness. Faking virtuous. Faking kindness. Faking achievements. Delusion. It's not just the norm in the mental clinic. It's everywhere. The be all and end all.

Limbo is the end, and it is the beginning, and then it ends again. Life and death and life. The snake eating its own tail for infinity.

The End.

I'm watching both of them from behind the double doors leading from the chilly main hallway to the cold courtyard. Envying them both for the way they sit in their motionless togetherness. There's nothing fake or forced in that naked, unspoken devotion to each other. Contentment. It's heartbreakingly beautiful. That kind of healthy love. The kind of love that isn't needy or insecure or selfish or addictively miserable. They say misery loves company, so why am I always so alone?

I do love my parents, but I'd rather not meet them. Talk with them. Today or any other day. They're like everyone else. They don't really understand. They want me to just get over it. Get better. Forget about her. Amelie. Move on. They can't understand because they've always had each other. They've never had to watch the other walk away. They've never lost. Never been devalued. Discarded. Painted black. Dead to someone they love.

Mum, Dad, I'm dead.

I hung myself when I was eight years old and everything after has been a coma dream. The life I might've lived flashing before my dying eyes as a lie in a piss-drenched hospital bed with tubes hanging from every orifice. None of this is real. It's a black-and-white episode of *The Twilight Zone*.

Submitted for your approval: The case of Vincent and Amelie…

Mum, Dad, I'm sorry. I'm not really here. I never was. You aborted me when I was a 10-week-old fetus.

These visitations in the clinic are only clairvoyance. Communing with the departed. Ouija board conversations. Small talk séances.

I've been an apparition since Amelie died, and every day I fade a little more. Soon, I'll be a thin silhouette cast by lamplight and burnt away by sleep. A particle of dust catching a glimmer of sun through a broken window in an abandoned, unfurnished ground-floor apartment and then gone.

I always feel worst when my parents finally do leave. Seeing their pained and hopeful faces, talking with them about Amelie, always leaves me feeling shittier than before they came. I know they love me, but each visit is like a hit and run that leaves me crippled in a stagnant-water ditch beside a midnight motorway.

Bertie appears down the corridor and staggers over to pester me for another cigarette. I toss him what's left in my packet and tell him to fuck off. He does.

I push open the heavy doors. Shuffle out across the cracked pavement towards the two people who fucked and made me. Who didn't abort me. I'm wearing ratty blue slippers and the ratty green bathrobe I've been wearing all day. Everyday. I don't feel like dressing properly most days. There's not much point anyway.

My muscles and bones ache as though I've been washed out to sea, treading water for days. Weeks. Months. I've not the energy to see them both, to talk about family shit. Brothers, sisters, cousins, aunties, uncles, and grandparents on the outside. The mentally proficient with their school exams, cookery books, new shoes, cancer scares, driving tests, lottery wins, divorces, promotions, bowel movements, birthdays, marriages, and babies. I just don't care. I don't want to know. But they came and I need to keep up the appearance that I *am* getting better. That I *am* trying. Making an effort. The treatments *are* working. I *didn't want to* die. Life isn't just a derelict, windowless room in a vacant house in an uninhabited city, in a skeletal world without

Amelie. I *am* happy and healthy. I *am* satisfied and just fucking *full* to the *brim* with *contentment. Life is fucking great.*

I hold out my hand in the air, saying, "Hello" like a Native American Indian making bead belts at a roadside stand in the shadow of a Canadian mountain. *"How?"*

My father spots me first and clears his throat, which I guess is a sign for my mother to wake from out of her deep funk and to keep up their own appearance of not being extremely uncomfortable, upset, bewildered, and disappointed with the whole situation.

"Hello, dear," Mum says, snapping her head up. Anyone would think she'd been caught napping or in silent prayer. Circles of deep gray go to black underneath her blue eyes. Irises too wide. She's nervous she's back where she is. Even though she comes every other week and she's just a visitor now. A name absentmindedly scribbled with a chewed biro pen in the visitors' book at the front desk. Her treatment successful. Her aching emptiness apparently filled. Her stalled heart shocked back into a cheerful beat. The life she tried to end, too, worth living now. The difference between us is—I'm not really sick. I don't need to get better.

"Hey, Mum." I nod. "Hello, Dad." I nod again.

They both appear much frailer every time they come to visit. Always momentarily snatching my breath away. We're all fading away together.

I'm not quite sure if I came into the clinic a month ago or a year ago. Time here has slowed for me but sped up for them. There are snow-white hairs, and carved wrinkles on their heads and faces. A physical fragility I can't ever remember being there before. My stomach drops, realizing if I don't die first, they will be dead before me, and I will have to mourn them like I have to mourn everything else. Like Amelie, they'll be gone. Dust. Everything you love dies. Everyone leaves you. Nothing means anything in the end. There will come a time when your name is uttered carelessly into a dwindling, twilight space for the very last time and it'll be as though you never existed at all. A character in a novel never written. A portrait never painted. A photograph undeveloped, untaken. A baby unborn.

My father drags over a plastic garden chair for me to sit down on in front of them. I'm to do a monologue for an audience of two. An audition. I'm to play a well-adjusted, healthy, happy young man ready to get back out there, into the big, bright world, kick ass and take names. The problem is I never could act. Kicked out of my GCSE drama class in secondary school for smoking behind the stage.

My head aches and each movement sends a shock of pain down my body—shock treatments of reality, but I let myself fall into the seat and light a cigarette. Cross my arms and legs. Uncross them. Cross them again. Scratch. Blink. Blow smoke at the passive gray sky. Avoid eye contact because, if I look into my parents' eyes for too long, I may burst into tears and no one wants that. Especially me.

"Does anyone want a coffee?" my father asks after only a few long moments of silence. Eager to break the awkwardness and disengage himself somehow.

"They've still only got the decaffeinated shit. We aren't allowed anything else. But you both already know that, right? Should do, the amount of time you've both spent in this courtyard," I say.

"I wish you wouldn't curse in front of your mother, Vincent." My father shakes his head and brushes at his mustache with a thick thumb. Then, "I'll just go and get some coffees. I'm parched. My mouth is as dry as an old leather boot. A coffee will do just the trick, I reckon." He gets up with newfound enthusiasm. His knees crack as he stands.

My mother and I watch him cross the courtyard with disinterest as he disappears through the main doors into the hallway, towards the cafeteria. Alone with my mother, I'm on a sinking ship. Waves crash over the stern. Debris float and sink. Cold ocean water laps over my feet. My guts. Rising to my throat. My mother probably feels the same. The whole courtyard is a poop deck on the Titanic. I clear my throat a couple of times like I'm getting ready to make a public speech or vomit.

She reaches out and gently squeezes my hand. Hands too hot. Tears cloudy in her bloodshot eyes.

For a moment, I am eight years old, having a brain scan or going to see another doctor.

TEN

My mother is driving me to a place that looks like my primary school, but it isn't.

She sits smoking, staring at the building through the windscreen after we park.

I count the cigarette butts in the ashtray. Four. I don't like that number. My grandmother told me it was bad luck and then she died from a heart attack.

We sit, waiting in the car for a long while. The engine clicks, clicks, clicks like raindrops on a tin roof and then my mother undoes our seatbelts, telling me it's time to go in.

We walk across the car park very slowly, hand in hand. There aren't any ghosts in this car park.

Inside the building, my mother speaks in hushed tones to the woman at a lime green reception desk. We sit in the waiting room that has many green plastic chairs and a fish tank with a single goldfish floating around in it. It smells like a dentist's office. I hate the dentist. I don't want a sticker as a swapsy for the teeth ripped from my mouth.

A girl with eyes like watery egg yolks in a frying pan and flaking bald patches on her scalp is sitting across from me. Kicking her legs back and forth. Her eyes are very blue. Blue is the color of the walls and the papery clothes of the woman standing with a clipboard in the doorway to an office.

The girl with the eyes like broken eggs keeps yanking out strands of her hair and letting them fall to the worn-out carpet like threads of gold from a picture book about fairy tales. Her mother keeps slapping at her small hand, and the girl puffs out her cheeks like the lonely goldfish in the large tank. She looks as though she's going to cry but doesn't. She doesn't stop pulling out her hair and I don't stop watching her. I wonder if the goldfish ate all the other fish in the tank. It looks fat enough and nasty enough. I don't like its face at all.

The woman with the clipboard, and papery blue clothes that make the same sound as the wind passing through the trees during the night, calls out my name.

My mother takes me by the fingers and leads me after the woman through a doorway and into another office. There, a tall, bald man who looks like a Halloween decoration smiles with square, yellow teeth and ruffles my hair like we're old friends. We aren't old friends. He doesn't know me. I wonder if he's one of the dirty old men my grandmother warned me about.

Creepy Halloween Man's room smells like dust and medication. There's a big, brown desk he sits behind. Many thick books the color of blood on the shelves. In the corner are colorful alphabet blocks scattered across a play mat. The blocks spell out **AMELIE**. He jabs a silver pen through the air at the blocks and, with a mouth that is small and round, he says I can play with them. I don't want to play with them. Just looking at the blocks makes my skin itchy underneath my sweater. Dirty. I know they're probably sticky from all the other children touching them. I don't want to play with things all the other kids have been using. I want toys that are just for me. Just mine. I say, "No, thank you," and move closer to my mother, who puts her hand on the back of my neck. Her fingers wrap tightly around the flesh, comforting.

My mother and the skeleton man talk and talk, and I stare and stare out the window. I see the top of a tree. The branches have no leaves and are like the blue veins in the back of my hands. A crow lands, hops, and perches. I would like a pet crow. One of my teachers, Mrs. Parsons, has a pet magpie. It fell out of the nest when it was a baby and she rescued it.

Later, when I yawn, the skeleton man gives me a large piece of white paper and a new pencil. He says I can draw anything I want. Whatever comes into my mind, he says.

I draw a picture of a cracked skull with a snake coiling itself through the black, hollow eye sockets and give it back to him. I feel proud of my sketch. It's cool. A tattoo I saw on the arm of one of my father's friends. The doctor looks at it for a long time, nodding. Tells me my picture is very good and then to go outside and wait. My mother watches me leave with a strange look in her eyes, like I am leaving her forever. She knows I'm dead, just like Grandma and all the ghosts in the car park. Just like Amelie.

The little girl is gone when I go back into the waiting room. Her gold hair still coiled like snakes on the carpet, catching the light. The waiting room vacant. The air feels weird.

I watch the lonely goldfish flap around in the green tank. Drowning. I am sad and don't know why. That girl yanking out her hair, unable to stop, is inside my brain like a horror movie. Her mother slapping at her. I pinch the skin on my hand until her ghostly face merges with the other things my head is crowded and cluttered like the attic at home. I pick up some of the little girl's hair and put it in the pocket of my jeans. It makes me feel a little better.

When my mother comes out of the room, her eyes and mouth are small like the doctor's. She says he thought I just had an overactive imagination. My mother says that means I think too much. I may need something called "counselling." She tuts. Mutters the bad words "bastard" and "shit" a few times and then apologizes to me.

She drives us home.

She smokes seven cigarettes. She cries five tears. I count them as they fall onto her denim jacket and make stains the color of rain. Sometimes my mother cries when she is eating dinner or when she is vacuuming the carpet. She tells me she just feels like crying sometimes. I wonder if she sees the black scribble in her head at night too. When she closes her eyes. I want to cry but I can't. All the tears collect in my stomach like when you put your hand over the plug hole in the sink and the water flows up and over the top, onto the floor. It makes me feel like I need to do a poop but, when I go to the toilet, nothing comes out, so the feeling never goes away. It's always there like rainwater in a muddy puddle. I am full of rainwater.

ELEVEN

I should feel guilty for putting my parents through all this. I don't though. I don't feel much of anything except a great loss. That's one of my problems, maybe.

We sit in silence, my mother and me, slowly blinking at each other and smoking.

"How are you doing lately, sweetheart?" My mother tries to sound cheerful.

I shrug with my mouth. Pulling the lips down. Wave my cigarette in a 50/50 motion.

"Have you talked with Katherine any more about..?" *Blah blah blah blah blah blah blah blah.* She sounds like the teacher from *Charlie* fucking *Brown.*

I stare at the sky. Try to remember what it looked like when I gazed up at it with Amelie. My mother drones on and on. I tune her out. I warned her there are things I will not fucking discuss. Don't want to fucking hear about. Or be asked about.

Finally, she changes the subject and stops twisting the knife into my brain.

I tune back into her wavelength.

"So, urm, have you done any of your writing recently, dear?" Her voice is wavering, flipping up at the end with fake positivity.

"Writing? Nah. What the hell would I even write about in this place?"

"What about the mystery novel you were writing before? That story sounded very interesting, dear. About the Hollywood actress that went missing in the '40s? Me and your dad thought it sounded like a great idea. Very interesting. Promising."

"No, what would be the fucking point of writing that now?" I say to myself as much as my mother.

"How about the poetry then? You writing any of those poems, Vincent?"

"I said I'm not writing anything, Ma."

"Oh, you should, dear. You were really good at writing stories and poetry, weren't you? All those people published you in their magazines. On the internet and that. Besides, it'll be…

What do they call it? *Therapeutic.* Yes, it'll be therapeutic. That's it! When your sister was here, she did coloring. You know, in those coloring books, only they're coloring books for adults, not for kiddies. You know the ones I mean. Really helped her to relax and that, they did. Would you like me to bring you some notebooks or something to write in next time we visit? How about a laptop? Are you allowed a laptop in here, dear?"

"No, it's all right, Mum. Don't worry about it. I can't write anything anyway. I can't do anything right now."

"Don't say that, dear."

"I don't feel like doing anything. Like I said, what's the point? Everything feels like it's lost its taste. It's like I can't taste anything anymore."

"The food is still *that* bad in here, is it?" She attempts a smile.

I know she's trying to joke, lighten the mood a little, but I go on the offensive anyway, because it's always easier. "No, no," I say. "Never fucking mind, Mum. You should know better than anyone what I'm talking about. For fuck sake."

"Don't get like that, dear. You know I can barely remember those days now. I got better. Put it all behind me. You'll be better soon, too. This is just a bump in the road. You have to try and stay positive. It does get better, I promise. You won't feel like this forever." She attempts to smile again, hopefully, encouragingly, the way I suppose all mothers attempt to for their fucked-up kids.

"Get me out of this place, Ma. I need to get out of here. I'll be better at home with you and Dad. I could have my own room again. The box room."

"Oh, Vincent, you know I'd love nothing more in the world than to walk out of here with you today and drive you home with us, but that's just not possible right now, dear. We would get into trouble and so would you."

"This is a mental health clinic, Mum. Not Alcatraz. You and Dad can do whatever you want. Take me out of here whenever you want."

"We've talked about *this* before, Vincent. You're here by court order. Please try and understand that."

"Fuck it then, just fuck it! Forget I asked."

"Don't get like that, Vincent. Please! You know we're all doing the best we can."

"Yeah, sure. Whatever. Forget it."

"Are you taking your medicine?"

"Fuck! Not *you* as well, Ma. Yeah, yeah, yeah. Sure, I'm taking all the pills they can shove down my fucking throat. And all my multivitamins, too. God forbid I forget to take my fucking meds."

We fall back to sitting in silence. I crush three more cigarette butts on the concrete and turn Amelie's last letter around in my fingertips when my father returns, balancing a tray with three plastic cups of milky coffee on it. I slide Amelie's suicide note back into my breast pocket with the photographs. Rubbing my hand over its outline like I've got indigestion.

"Sorry for the wait, there was a bit of a queue in the canteen, and I got talking with that Iranian chap," my father says.

We sip at the lukewarm, flavorless coffee and peer around at everything but each other's wincing faces. Making eye contact is like staring directly into bloody, pus-filled wounds. Mortal injuries. Gangrenous. Seeping. Weeping. It's painful and we avoid it for as long as we possibly can. Birdsong somewhere distant is almost deafening. I wonder if Katherine is doing another one of her group therapy sessions. I pick at threads of cotton from my bathrobe and roll them up into balls between my thumb and forefinger before flicking them away. Glancing at my watch like I've got somewhere important to be.

"You're still wearing the wristwatch Amelie gave you then, Vincent. Has Katherine…"

"I asked him that earlier," Mum brightly chimes in.

I scrunch up my eyes, shaking my head until I'm dizzy. Images try to shove their way into my mind. I push them away. Try to go back in time. Somewhere good.

A hand on my shoulder. I slowly turn to see my father's face. Weathered and worry-lined.

"Are you all right, Vincent?"

"What?"

"Are you all right? You drifted off."

"No, I'm not all right. Did you tell Nurse Ratched I wasn't a Muslim?" I croak.

"Who?" my father asks, frowning.

"*Katherine*, the boss bitch, the head shrink. Did you tell her?"

"Yes, Vincent. We told her," my mother answers. She asked us about it last week—and don't talk about her like that. She's trying her best to help you, isn't she?"

My father asks, "You don't even believe in God, Vincent. What the hell did you tell them you were a Muslim for?"

"Look, it doesn't really matter now. Just don't tell them anything else. I don't want you guys talking to Nurse Ratched anymore. Nothing. Don't tell her anything."

"Well, what are we supposed to do if she asks us something? We *have* to talk with her to help you," Mum says.

"It's not helping me though. It's making things much more difficult. Whose side are you on anyway? I'm your *son* for fuck sake."

"Can't you see everyone is just trying to help you?" my parents say together. It sounds scripted. Rehearsed. I wonder who's acting now or if it's an ensemble act. A comedy sketch. An actor's improv afternoon at the clinic.

I keep my mouth shut. Light another cigarette even though I don't want one and cross my arms and lean back, staring at a pink, fleshy scar on my right knuckle. Puffing gray smoke up towards a sky the color of a cataract. "Ma, did you bring me what I asked for?" I glance around to make sure no one else can hear.

The courtyard is desolate except for Bertie examining dead roses. Holding the black petals in the palms of his quivering hands and mumbling to himself.

My father scratches at his Roman nose with a pinkie, eyes barely contained within his face. He hisses underneath his breath, "No, she bloody well didn't! What the hell were you thinking? Asking your mother to bring you drugs? LSD for Christ's sake!"

My mother looks down as though she has failed me. She has. "I'm sorry, Vincent. I couldn't."

"What the hell do you want to take acid for, anyway? That's partly the reason why you're in this place, probably. All those drugs you were doing in secondary school and all the drinking. It's only made things worse."

"I was only smoking weed in secondary school and I wasn't drinking *that* much."

"Exactly! The bloody marijuana! It's done this to you. Read about it in the newspaper. Makes people mentally ill. Causes schizophrenia."

"Which tabloid newspaper did you read that in, dad? *The Sun* or *The Daily Sport*?"

"Doesn't matter where I read it. It's a fact, marijuana makes people sick in the head."

"Oh, it's the weed I smoked years ago and not the fact Amelie is fucking dead?"

My father sighs heavily, massages his deeply lined temples with his knuckles and looks at my mother, shrugging, shaking his head.

My mother passes me a plastic bag with cartons of cigarettes and comics inside. I want to tell her I'm not an eight-year-old anymore, I don't read comics, I'm a grown man. I'd like to tell her that I love her, too. That I'm sorry for being a prick all the time. That I can't seem to control myself, my rusty see-saw feelings, my tail-spin thoughts. But I don't say those things either. It feels cheap. Forced. Expected. I go back to not saying anything. Just nodding like one of those toy dogs in the backs of cars or a therapist pretending to listen. I slide the bag down on the cracked concrete underneath my chair. The breeze catching at the plastic makes noises like the death rattle in the throat of a geriatric patient.

I finally ask the question that has been hanging from the tip of my tongue like a fleshy growth since I'd first sat down. "Have you heard anything from Amelie's mum yet?"

My mother and father exchange another long look. My father coughs out a "No." Rolling his eyes. He sounds annoyed. On edge. It pisses me off.

Mother pulls at her fingers, wringing her hands.

They both turn in unison to stare towards the entrance as though contemplating escape. I start scratching at my face and neck. Skin feverish. Anger boiling up from the pit of my stomach. I am a man made from tinder. The wicker man burning up. I am a house fire. "What? Still nothing? I can't fucking believe this. If I could speak to someone close to Amelie, it would help a lot. Everyone's always droning on about *helping me, helping me, helping me*. So fucking *help me*! *Help me* get some kind of fucking closure here."

My father glares down into his empty coffee cup. My mother tries to change the subject by stuttering something about one of my siblings. The happier one. The mentally healthy one. The unscathed one. "Maria finished her master's degree… She, she, she, she, told me to tell you…" my mother stutters.

"I don't give a fuck about any of that! Don't try to change the fucking topic, Mum. Why the fuck hasn't she tried to contact me, huh? *Her daughter, my girlfriend,* fucking killed herself. You would have thought she'd send me a fucking letter at least. Something! She blames me, I know it. I don't blame her. She convinced Amelie to have an abortion, as well. It wasn't just me. I've been a mess since Amelie went. She could reach out, at least. The selfish fucking cunt. Cunts!"

My father inhales through gritted, chipped teeth. Massaging the bridge of his nose, a man with a migraine from staring at a computer screen for too long. "Son, you've had problems for a number of years. You needed help even before that bloody girl came along. From since you were a kid, you've had problems. Now you need to sort your head out and get yourself together. Get your self-respect back. And stop the cursing in front of your mother, please."

"That's complete bullshit. I was fine. Why do you both even come here? To just sit there, bullshitting me? Is that it? Did Katherine put you up to this? She *did,* didn't she?"

"Vincent, you're shouting. Lower your voice or you'll get the staff worried. Please." My mother's hand quivers over her mouth. I wonder if she's signaling Katherine somehow.

"Fuck the staff! Fuck Katherine. Fuck Michael. Fuck Greg."

"Who are you talking about now? Michael and Greg who?" My mother looks around, confused.

"Amelie's mother. The heartless cunt really hasn't tried to contact you *at all?*"

"Why would she, Vincent?" My father sighs.

"What do you fucking mean *why?* It's obvious *why!*"

"Please, Vincent, please." My mother's tears run jagged from the corners of her pink eyes, down to the deeply lined edges of her mouth.

One of the support staff strolls over behind me, grinning like a reptilian. "Everything all right over here, is it?"

"Fine! Fine!" My parents smile coldly too.

Now everyone's smiling but me. "No, not fine. Not fine at all. Amelie is *dead*. She's *dead!* She fucking killed herself because of *me!* Because of *me!* How the fuck is anything fine? You silly, little nurse cunt! Fuck off!" My voice breaks. High-pitched like an eight-year-old wheezing, fading out.

"Oh, Vincent, please, please, you need to forget about that selfish little bitch. She left you! You need to accept..." My mother weeps hysterically.

Everyone is shouting words at me.

I block out all the things they say. Pushing my palms hard over my ears. A migraine of images explodes at the back of my skull. Screwing my eyes up so tightly, I can't even see their wrinkled mouths opening and closing.

None of this is real.

Then I'm standing, lifting the plastic garden chair above my head and smashing it down on the courtyard floor. Plastic shards scatter, dirty white. I'm calling my parents cunts.

My mother is wailing. My father's holding her close.

Michael and Greg appear and attempt to put my arms in a judo lock behind my back.

I fight. Refusing to relax or be restrained. I'm screaming.

Katherine and the others are here too now.

I'm surrounded by gaping, ugly faces. Masks. Plastic soles scraping over gritty cement. Hands grabbing at me. Fingers painfully pressing into my flesh.

Father pulling my mourning mother away.

I'm yelling Amelie's name into a blurred void.

A prick of a needle.

Body heavy and awkward.

And...

I close my eyes into the bright white nothing.

It's beautiful.

TWELVE

I'm sat in a pub on Camden High Street.

World's End.

The end of the world.

My world.

I come here after work every night.

It's a dive, the drinks are a rip-off, and it stinks, but it's popular. I like the atmosphere.

Tonight, there's a dog-eared, gold banner wilted over the bar, stating, **Sixties Night.**

Groups huddle in intimate clusters of friendly, glowing faces. Hipsters, Rockers, students, and coked-up suits rub shoulders. The air is alive with electricity and drunken conversation.

I cast my eyes over the ocean of heads and momentarily wish I had friends of my own. I try to remember what happened to them. Mind's blank. Not sure I ever really had any. Never felt as though I've belonged to anything. Anywhere. Not a lone wolf, more of a street stray.

Poor me. Poor me. Pour me another drink.

The music is pretty great. I collect old LPs and know a lot of the songs being played. Every so often move my lips to sing along. I'm in a good mood, but slightly nervous. I wipe sweaty palms on the legs of my jeans and gulp down the remnants of my third drink. That pleasant liquor candle burning in the throat and chest.

Waiting.

Waiting for a *deux ex machina.*

My *deux ex machina.*

I just don't know it yet.

A gang of pissed-up girls fall through the front doors, laughing. All dressed-up in bubblegum pink, imitating the women from the movie *Grease.* It's a hen party for the loud, moon-faced, busty brunette leading the pack, waving a three-foot purple dildo in the air. I don't know that yet either, of course. I'll find that out when I strike up a halfhearted conversation with her best friend, the cute redhead with the silver lip ring, swaying at the bar. By that time, I'll only be paying half a mind to what she's shouting in my ear, because my focus will be on Amelie, who has just strolled into the pub, glancing around apprehensively, a crookedly unsure shimmer touching the corners of her dark eyes. I know it's a hackney expression, but she really does stop my breath.

Suddenly, I'm drowning in the sea of noise that is her. Amelie.

I run my fingers through my hair and stand up quickly. The glasses on the table rattle crazily. A standing ovation for a show that hasn't even started yet.

This stunning girl's looking across the crowd, the faces, for *me*. Coming to meet *me*. I feel taller. Bigger. I've grown a few more inches. I'm Frank Fucking Sinatra.

Still running fingers through my hair, I murmur to myself not to fuck this up and wave her over, grinning like an idiot savant. Every light in the bar draws on her, illuminating the shape of her. Her curves. The way she moves. I remind myself to breathe. Inhale. Exhale.

The deejay starts playing Elvis' "Can't Help Falling in Love." The smirk grows into a smile, breaking out across my face. Skin pulled tight. Muscles in my cheek twitching. *Been a while since I smiled like this.* Been a while since I had something resembling promise. Some real unbelievable *Mills & Boon* shit. Can't quite believe my luck.

I'm not bad looking. Work out. Getting laid was always pretty easy. But that was with the kind of women who would go home with anyone, rather than go home alone and face the morning themselves. Women with just as much baggage as me. Awkward mornings drinking other people's coffee, smoking their cigarettes, looking around their flats, the photographs in frames, the books on their shelves. Watching them disinterestedly as they rush around their bedroom to get ready for work or to pick the kids up from Grandma's house. Or grabbing their dress, their earrings from cheap motel floors, to get home before their spouses wonder where they are. There was never any kind of promise there. With those women. It was a nightcap. A taxi ride to somewhere transient. A treading of water.

Those one night stands are like pilots circling above the runway because they aren't ready to touchdown yet. Afraid to crash and burn. Time filler. And that's okay, but there are no promises to be made. No promises to be seen. Agreements to use each other for the night because there are some nights that have claws and teeth and pick off the solitary straggler.

I know as soon as I first glimpse Amelie through the crowd that she isn't going to be like any of the others before her. Promise. Something supernatural, like fate. As though I've been slumped in this pub my entire life, waiting for her to push through the crowd to me. Like I said, Real *Mills & Boon* shit.

The bar and the crowds blur in and out of sync. Everything is cast in static shadow but Amelie. I could be in a movie theater, watching her up there on the silver screen.

She looks like Marilyn Monroe. Heart-shaped face. Stars in those limpid, almond eyes of hers. No, not mere stars. Planets. She holds planets in the darkness of her eyes.

I'm still short of breath, panting like a mutt chasing cars in rush-hour traffic.

She's wearing a close-fitting emerald dress with buttons down the front. The first few are undone, showing off her creamy throat and cleavage that anchors a hook in my prick. Hem of her dress reveals the kind of thighs that break the suicidal hearts of poets and pickpockets. Long, wavy, peroxide-blonde hair worn down and parted to the side. The kind of mouth that pouts that she's gotten her way her entire life. The way her hips and arse sway underneath the fabric of her dress causes me to sit down and stand back up.

Pure sex radiates from her. A scolding steam burning everyone in proximity to her.

In my head, I'm thanking gods I've never believed in.

I'm completely and pleasantly pussy-whipped before she's uttered a single word.

Amelie has that kind of power.

Every guy in the place feels the same way I do. Grasping half-full glasses of warm lager halfway from their faces. Stupefied. Shocked and awed. The women too. Cupid just went high school shooter on the whole pub. It's a bloody and beautiful massacre.

We lock eyes and it's a sawn-off shotgun blast to my chest cavity. *POW!*

She's smiling at *me*.

No, that's wrong. She doesn't smile. She beams. As though she's just told herself a dirty joke or she knows something special that I don't, and she probably does.

We are both actors on a stage now. The audience gone forever dark. Infinitely silent. Endlessly mute.

This is our world now. Our movie to play out. Our show.

She cups a hand around her plump lips and shouts over the pounding music, "You're Vincent, right?" Her perfume almost knocks me off my feet. Coco by Chanel, but I don't know that yet.

"Yeah, Amelie?" I shout back, softly placing my hand on her side, just under and to the side of her left breast. The fabric of the dress underneath my fingertips. Lips close to her ear. Invading her personal space because I want to conquer it and every single inch of her. Lick every centimeter of her.

All I can smell is that perfume and her fruity hair conditioner. My stomach pleasurably tightens. All knotted up like a noose.

"Yes!"

"Nice to meet you!"

"Great to meet you too, Vincent!"

I gesture down to the table, and she slides into the seat with poised confidence, her back to the bar. This is my memory, so I know what she's drinking but ask anyway because some memories shouldn't be changed. I don't want to change. Don't want to alter anything about this night.

Our first night.

The first memory.

I'm letting it play out like a favorite song listened to until you've learnt every single word, chord, riff, and bar.

"What do you want to drink?"

She plays with the menu, sliding it around in circles on the tabletop, chewing at her bottom lip. Crossing her legs high, shuffling her arse deeper into the imitation leather seat. Pulling the hem of her dress down a little. She's nervous, too. Wearing mismatched jewelry. Silver and gold rings on every finger. Bracelets of beads and precious metal dangling from her wrists. Eye contact drifting like cigarette smoke. I catch a long glimpse of the top of her thigh, and it sends a pulse of electricity through my body like I'm lying on the street somewhere with paramedics shocking me to life with a defibrillator. No longer a flat line. I feel alive and hyperaware.

"I'll have a sangria, I guess. Thank you, Vincent."

This is something Amelie will always do. Punctuate each of her sentences with my name like a *coup de grace* bullet through the head. I love the way she says my name in her American accent. The intonation on *cent*. The breathy way it rolls up and off the tip of her tongue.

"Okay, *señorita*," I say.

Her eyebrows flash confused. Not getting the lame joke.

I'll explain it in passing the next morning over breakfast, and she'll tell me she assumed I thought she was Spanish and we'll both cringe a little and laugh about it the way the best morning-afters go.

The music cuts out. Skips into another song. Time gone. Another song.

Fast forward. Stop. Pause. Play.

I'm sitting again. Collections of empty glasses clustered in front of us. The pub is emptier, the crowds grown thin. Bar staff beginning to wipe down tables. Amelie's mobile phone lights up every so often with text message notifications and then incoming calls that cause the phone to vibrate madly. Amelie rolls her eyes and turns the mobile screen face-down.

"My stalker." She cringes.

"You've got a stalker? Who is it?"

"Just some clingy guy who I dated for a little a while back. He got super possessive and jealous, so I ended things. He's an asshole. Don't worry about it. It's nothing. Really." This should have been a sign. An omen for my future. One day I would be the person calling. The name on the ignored screen.

In the dim lighting, my eyes are drawn to a few smooth, shiny scars on her left arm. These imperfections make her all the more beautiful to me. I don't know why. "What are these?" I take the excuse to touch her flesh.

"Oh, I have an angry cat." She grimaces and crosses her arms.

"Earth Angel" by the Penguins starts playing. A song which I have on vinyl, made famous by the movie *Back to the Future*, I tell her to change the subject.

"I haven't seen it," she giggles, embarrassed. Stalker and scars forgotten. Stirring the ice in her glass with an orange straw.

"You're seriously telling me you haven't seen *Back to the Future*?" I'm starting to slur a little. Speaking slowly to control it. Enunciating every syllable, so I don't come across as a lightweight idiot who can't hold his liquor.

She slowly sucks on the straw, raises her eyebrows, and locks eye contact. Swallows, says, "No. Should I, Vincent?"

I lean further over the sticky table. Moving my arms closer. My face closer. I can feel her hot breath on my lips. "Yeah, you should. It's a classic, of course. You should come over to my place and watch it." I'm pushing my luck, but it feels right. I know it's right.

"I will if *you* want me to, Vincent. Do you *want* me to?"

"Oh, I definitely want you to."

The eye contact lingers longer.

Cupid pushes the barrel of a shotgun against my temple and performs the aforementioned *coup de grace*.

"You're much cooler than the photo you sent me. I didn't realize you have so many tattoos. You're covered, and it's a good thing though, because I love tattoos. I want one *so, so bad*." Even the way she speaks makes me hard. She traces the ink embedded in my right arm, sending a throbbing pulse down my chest and stomach, straight to the tip of my dick.

"Are you flirting with me, Amelie, or are you just drunk?" A cheesy question, I know, but at this point I don't give a fuck about anything anymore.

She gazes dead into my eyes and says, "Yeah, I'm flirting. How's it working out for you, Vin?"

"Hell, it's working out pretty fucking great, Amelie."

"Good, I hope so." She beams again.

I'm punch-drunk.

Promise.

Looking back on it, Amelie had the scalpel precision of a heart surgeon when it came to seduction. I never stood a chance. Like fishing in a barrel. With hand grenades. She mirrored my words and gestures the whole night through. Finished my sentences. Laughed at all my lame jokes. Touched me whenever she wanted to emphasize a word. Leaned forward into me. Gave me glimpses of her body. Let me inhale the scents of her perfume mixed with her sweat. Letting me know I could have it all. She was sex personified. Every single thing about her screamed it. But there was a fragility about her too. As though she was telling me she needed me to save her without saying a word. She seduced me with her needfulness just as much she did her body and her mind.

Later, lying in the bed, we jokingly argued about who came onto who first. It was something we would tease each other about through the duration of our time together. I was always sure it was Amelie, but, even to this day, I'll never understand what a woman as beautiful as her ever saw in a guy like me. A broke underachiever with mental problems and a propensity to drink to excess. The whole time we were together, I was always waiting for the catch. The twist. The bucket of pig's blood to fall over my head in front of a laughing crowd.

"And when did she tell you that she was married? Wasn't *that* at least some kind of a twist? A catch?"

I glance to my right. Katherine's sitting at the next table. She's drinking what smells like milky tea. It's as though I've just switched channels on a television set and the pub has become Katherine's office. A mahogany desk with a telephone and a personal computer neatly arranged around thick, manila files. A large potted plant in the corner. One of those annoying chrome-swinging-ball things where the motion never stops and therapists and school principals compulsively put them on their desks. A small crack in the wall plaster above the computer console. The screen is open to a popular social media website. Someone's downloaded photographs. A beach somewhere. Smiles. Happiness captured in snapshots and splashed onto the internet for all to see.

My left eye twitches. My head aches. I look away. "What are you doing here?" I ask her.

"I'm sorry, Vincent?" She frowns at me. Raising her chin to the side.

"I mean, what were we talking about, again? I seem to have lost my train of thought here. Too tired, maybe."

"Have you been having trouble sleeping?" She reaches towards the table and the pen there.

"No, no, I'm sleeping fine. Fine. Sleeping isn't the problem. It's the waking up… What I'm trying to say is, I just sometimes lose my train of thought. That's all."

"We're in the middle of a session right now, Vincent. We were talking about what happened yesterday, when your parents were here visiting you. Discussing possible triggering moments, triggering situations. Talking about Amelie. You were telling me about the first night you met her. Are you all right? Would you like to take a break a moment? Have a drink of water?"

"No, I'm fine. Just the drugs you people give me make things jumbled and confused." I stare. I blink. I close my eyes.

I'm in the bar again.

I turn back to look at Amelie. My face is too hot. Itchy. Embarrassed. She's talking about all her favorite places she's traveled and doesn't seem to notice Katherine at all.

Why should she? This is just a memory, I have to keep reminding myself.

I'm becoming more confused about what exactly *it is* I'm recollecting. Maybe Katherine and the office are the memories, the things I'm struggling to remember. The past and the future are two sides of the same coin, tossed in the air. Spinning erratically.

Am I in the past dreaming of the future or in the future dreaming of the past?

Two sides of the same rusty, old coin.

Amelie and me.

Fucking and fighting.

Loving and hating.

Living and dying.

Alive and dead.

In Limbo.

Infinitely.

"Vincent?" Katherine slurps at her tea, smacking her lips and sighing satisfactorily like a fat cat with a magpie in its jaws.

I'm dizzy, motion sick, but wave my hand in circles like, *Let's go, let's go*, stuttering at her that I'm fine to go on.

"Okay, so, how about Amelie? Did she tell you she had a husband on the first night you met?" she asks.

"Not a husband," I shrug and shake my head. The headache scratches around within the walls of my skull, a rodent in violent protest.

"Not a husband?"

"Yes, not a husband. *A fiancé*. She was engaged, not married. That's what she told me."

Katherine is trying to catch me out. Last session, I lied and told her Amelie wasn't married. I don't know why I lied, but sometimes it's comforting to control the narrative.

Katherine flicks through her fat notebook, frowning down at her notes. "Ah yes, I do apologize, Vincent. My mistake. *A fiancé*. Did she tell you about him that first night? The fiancé?"

"Yeah," I mutter. "I already told you all that. Last session."

"What were your thoughts when she told you about him?" Katherine asks.

THIRTEEN

Amelie reaches over to me, stroking my arm. Squeezing my flesh between her fingertips. "Vincent, I'm just going to say it! I really like you so much already, so, I guess, I should really be honest about something. I have a husband, back in the US. I mean, I'm married, but I'm really unhappy with him. He isn't nice to me at all." She flicks threads of hair over her shoulder. Purses her cherry red lips into a 0 shape. They glisten. Moist in the dim bar lights.

A blowjob from her would place me halfway from Heaven. I down the remnants of another drink and tell myself to make the next round my last. If I'm about to get lucky, it'll be just my shitty luck to vomit or get whiskey dick and ruin the whole damn thing. Amelie holds out her petite hand and fingers a cheap wedding ring hidden amongst the assorted rings. I'm more interested in the emerald polish on her fingertips. Imagining how they feel across my flesh. Down my back and across my chest.

"So, while you think about that little bombshell, it's my turn to get the drinks, isn't it, Vincent? You want the same? I think they'll call for last orders soon anyway." She gets up, smiling, and places that ringed hand on the back of my neck to send hot shivers down my spine. I want her so badly; my whole body is feverish with it.

I've already forgotten what she said about the fiancé. Husband. She might as well have told me that it rained yesterday for all it mattered. I already decided I wanted her, and I wasn't going to let something like a fiancé, husband…her marriage… or whatever else fuck that up.

After the bell for last orders is well past rung, I place my hand on the small of her back and guide her out into a night humming electric with expectations and streetlights.

Walking her home, we finally kiss, jumping into it headfirst, clumsy, and raw. Our bodies press hard into the curves of each other. Pull at each other impatiently, stepping on toes, into an alley.

We fuck against a crumbling brick wall, behind a dumpster. Her dress up around her waist, panties pulled to the side, and my jeans around my ankles. Surrounded by trash, draped in darkness underneath a drizzling rain. It's the most passionate sex I'd ever had in my life until that point. Amelie burns with a kind of hunger that reaches out to feed like an open flame. Fiercely holding me against her and gripping my flesh as though she'll never want to let me go. I feel truly wanted. Needed. A loser my whole life, I feel like I'm finally winning something I want to win.

I don't even wear a rubber. Come inside her. She could give me every disease under the sun—I just don't care. I would accept them all, gratefully.

I do.

"I see. Vincent, going back to her previous relationship a little more, what were your thoughts about that when she told you?" Katherine asks again. Jarring me back into the office.

I use a potted plant in the corner as an anchor to the here and now and glare at it. Exhaling until I'm out of breath then inhaling deeply. "My thoughts about what exactly?" I sigh, exasperated at the potted plant.

"What were your thoughts when she told you about the *fiancé?*" Katherine repeats. *A broken record.*

I notice a crack in the plaster above the computer desk. It's grown a few inches longer. Branching out. Spreading like a broken artery across the wall. A dead tree in a bleak winter white. Within the grim slit, I glimpse the darkness within. I am staring into a reflection of midnight glass. An abyss that has my eyes, my mouth, my cheeks, my nose, my face. "It was just a hook up in the beginning. Wasn't a date or anything. We didn't know it was going to be serious like it turned out to be." I rub my palms on the front of my bathrobe. Placing a hand to my chest, where the photographs and Amelie's letter are. The crack above the PC shortens in length again. I rub my eyes and blink. Lean back in the chair, pulling the bathrobe around myself. Sweat pours down my torso. Droplets as fat as rain sliding from my armpits, down my sides, into the waistband of my jockey shorts.

The crack rips through the wall plaster, almost reaching the ceiling.

"And Amelie? What about her? She was just looking for a *hook up?*"

"Well, yeah. I guess. She'd been living in London for a year on a work placement course or something and she wanted to meet people. I don't know."

"She was living here with her *fiancé?*"

"No, he was in back in California. She'd lived with him over there for a few years before she came to London. But like I said already, I don't really know."

"I want to know what you thought about that, Vincent." Katherine makes notes in a manila folder that has my name typed on the front. The sound of the pen nib on the paper is erratic.

I wonder what she's writing. "Thought about what?" I ask the potted plant again.

"She had a husband, I mean fiancé, who she lived with for three years in California—yet she was meeting you under the pretense that she didn't have anyone."

"There wasn't any kind of *pretense.* You're beginning to sound a bit like a priest. I don't mean to sound rude, but you're not how I expect a therapist to sound at all. All these questions about shit that doesn't even matter. Are you writing my biography or what? Look, to answer your question, I didn't give a shit about any of that stuff. It's not like we knew we were planning to have a long affair. It just happened, I guess. We didn't care. Go ahead and write all that down in your manila folder. That's what you wanted to hear, isn't it?"

"Okay, so why? Why didn't you care?"

"Because we really hit it off. Amelie and me. Look, I'd signed up to this personals website and then forgotten all about it until Amelie messaged me with a photograph. She was beautiful. A stunner. I mean, a real knockout. We exchanged a couple of emails, liked the sound of each other, I suppose, so we decided to meet. That's it."

"You didn't think it was strange she was meeting guys from the internet in bars at night even though she had a *fiancé* waiting for her back in California?"

"No, and why do you have to say it like that? What are you? A monk? I told you already, I was fucking around the same way for a while. And, I already said, to be completely honest, I didn't give a shit about her fiancé."

"Why do you say that?"

"She told me he was abusive."

"And you chose to take her word on that?"

"Of course I did. What do you mean? Why wouldn't I?"

"What else did you think about her husband?"

"I don't know. Not a lot. He was an abusive piece of shit and I thought he was an idiot. To use the American term: a sucker. A chump. He had an amazing woman like Amelie, and he let her go. He should've made more of an effort. Tried harder to keep her."

"Like you felt you did?"

You fucking bitch. "Yeah, yeah, sure, just like me. She told me all about the way he treated her. Said he was violent. A real piece of shit. So, fuck that guy. He didn't deserve her. Why do you keep asking questions about all this kind of stuff? It's not relevant to anything now."

"Well, it's relevant to Amelie and she is a big part of the reason why you're an in-patient here at the clinic, Vincent. I'm just trying to understand what kind of a person you thought she was." She folds the manila envelope and lays it in her lap. Pushes the spectacles up her nose and thoughtfully nods to me. Doing one of those glum smiles where you pull your lips back into your mouth. A grim little slit. A self-harm scar. Waiting for me to say something. To spill my guts.

I close my eyes to show her I'm not playing her game. I'll run the clock down.

"You said, she told you her partner was violent. She told you about a stalker ex-affair partner. Did you feel compelled to look after her? Perhaps became fixated on the idea that you needed to save her? Protect her?"

"I wouldn't say *fixated*, but yeah, I guess I did."

"You briefly mentioned your mother's own battle with mental health. Often, boys who grow up in households with unhappy or depressed mothers find themselves in adulthood attracted to women who they feel need saving. Finding themselves in relationships with women who are difficult to please. Do you know about something called borderline personality disorder, Vincent?"

"Stop." I wave my hand in a chopping motion in front of my throat.

"What's wrong, Vincent?"

"I've told you before, I'm not going to talk about my mother or have her pulled into these sessions. Is that all they teach you in therapist school? Blame someone else? It's fucking lame. Blame the mother, right? What's that? The school of Freud."

"You're very protective of your mother."

"Maybe all sons are. I don't know."

"Did Amelie have children?"

"No!"

"Relax, Vincent." She puts her palms out, as if to calm me. Shuffling her ass deeper into the seat.

"We already talked about *that* as well. Why are you asking again when you already know the answers? Are you fucking with me? This enjoyable for you or something?"

"You know we have to discuss these things, Vincent."

"Over and over and over again?" I croak.

"You're avoiding key issues we need to resolve, Vincent."

You fucking bitch.

"Did you and Amelie have intercourse that first night?"

"What? No. Amelie wasn't like *that.*"

"Wasn't she?"

You fucking bitch.

She holds eye contact with me too long. A shiver rattles its way down my spine.

"Beatrice thinks I put Amelie up on a pedestal. Is that what you're getting at, too?"

"What do you think, Vincent? Do you think you put her up on a pedestal?"

I shrug. "Doesn't everyone do that? Put the people they love up on a pedestal?"

"What do you think were some of Amelie's positive points, Vincent?"

"That's easy," I say. Counting them off on my fingers. "She's beautiful. Really stunning. And she really made me laugh. I mean, she was really funny when she wanted to be. Could've been a comedian if she'd wanted. She had a high sex drive, like me. Wanted to do it everywhere, anytime. Wanted to try everything. She was generous with everything she had. She was completely focused on me. She was probably the smartest woman I've ever met, too. Real witty. And, man, could she drink.

We had this thing going, a competition of who could find the worst dive bar in London, and we'd go to those places on our date nights. Real shit holes. Get completely wasted. Take the piss out of the barflies and locals. It was pretty hilarious, but I guess you had to be there."

Katherine shifts in the chair, leans back. The joints squeal. *"She's beautiful."* Katherine raises her pencil-thin eyebrows.

"Yeah, that's what I said."

"You didn't say 'She *was* beautiful.' You said, 'She *is* beautiful.' Why, Vincent?" Katherine has that hungry glint in her eyes.

I shift my weight in the chair. "What's that plant there? In the corner? Amelie's mother had the same plant in her home. I saw it. When I went to New Jersey with Amelie. I just remembered it," I say, waving my hand at the plant like it's a rope and I'm drowning.

"You like it, Vincent?"

"Yeah, sure, I guess so."

She swivels around in her chair to nod at the blinding light radiating from the computer screen. The shit-eating grins of the happy family. Someone's profile picture. "Would you like to use my computer, Vincent? You could look it up on the internet."

I push myself deeper into my seat, "No! No, I don't want to."

"Do you use social media, Vincent?"

"No! No, I don't."

"Really, how come? I thought everybody uses social media nowadays. Keeping in touch with old friends. Stuff like that."

"No, I don't like social media. It's all bullshit."

"Why do you feel that way, Vincent?"

"Fuck it. I just wanted to know the name of the fucking plant. Not take a fucking survey on internet usage." Out of breath. Panting out words. I sit on my hands.

"Calm down, please, Vincent."

"I am *calm.* Just tell me the name of the plant or don't. I don't really give a shit either way."

"It's called a bird of paradise, Vincent."

I finally breathe out. "Bird of Paradise, huh? That's a cool-sounding name. Was it expensive? It looks pretty expensive, as far as plants go. Amelie's mother didn't seem very well-off, though."

Katherine jabs her pen at the clock on the wall. "Vincent, okay, we're getting slightly off point here and we're pushed for time. How would you feel if we tried something a little more, how should I put it, hands-on with your therapy?"

"Like electric shock treatments, Nurse Ratched?" I wink. A trickle of sweat runs down my face.

She guffaws. "Ha-ha! Very funny, Vincent. No, something more like an intervention. Something with lots of positive points, but fewer negatives." She trails off, twisting around to scribble a note in the open diary on her desk.

"An intervention? Like for alcoholics? I don't really give a shit about negative points anymore, so, whatever, I guess." I shrug and scratch my head.

"How about Amelie's negative points? Let's go back to her, shall we? Do you think she had any?"

"Sure. Everybody does, don't they? Nobody's perfect."

She leans back even further into her chair. The joints squeal in pain and I wonder if the chair's going to break. Katherine seems oblivious. Slurping more tea. Waiting for me to go on.

I glance at the crack on the wall and see it's gone now. The wall smooth and bare. The crack was never there to begin with. "Negative points." I scratch at my face. "Amelie's negative points."

A few months after the abortion.

My birthday.

I remember.

Sitting in a cigar bar by the window, on a side street in Mayfair. Watching the traffic drift by. The color of the sky fatigued yellow, same for the sun slouching across city cement and glass. Compulsively checking the time on my wristwatch and mobile phone every few minutes like a crackhead because my glass is empty, the cigars long ago crushed in a copper ashtray, and I don't know what else to do with myself. This void, meaningless time. Amelie isn't here. I don't know where she is.

Waiting for her to arrive. She's late. Already over an hour, and the truth is, I know deep down in my heart that she isn't coming.

Her phone's switched off. Going to voicemail. I've left three messages and texted her more than I should have. Starting to look needy and desperate. Trembling. Palsied. No, I feel way past needy and desperate. This is delirium tremens. The DTs. Weak as hell and I hate myself for it. Weak for Amelie and I hate her for that, too.

Hours before, we argued about the same thing as we did after the termination: how she wanted the baby, and I didn't. She'd slammed the front door to my apartment and ran off, shouting that she was going to jump off a bridge. Throw herself into traffic. She wanted to die, she said. I let her go. Used to the constant, hollow suicide threats. I should've gone after her, but I didn't. I wanted to prove a point to myself—and now the point is proven, I regret it. Can't even remember what it is I wanted to prove. Slumped in the cigar bar, acid boiling in my guts—eating its way through my stomach walls and splashing up into my chest cavity.

After this evening, I will never come to this cigar bar again. Tonight's the night that will cripple me. Whenever I find myself in the proximity of this place, I'll go out of my way to avoid the slightest glimpse of the building. The exterior detonating waves of nausea, vertigo and sweat-drenched anxiety inside my head and guts. My mental snapshot of the front windows is like rubbing powdered glass into rotten wounds. In time, I'll come to avoid this whole area of London.

My 27th birthday.

The anniversary of my birth.

Proof of life.

I am alive. I'm not dead.

A few months after the abortion of our child. This evening is supposed to be a chance for normalcy, for fresh starts. Celebrations. Remedies. Instead, from this moment forward, I'll hobble through the months, emotionally wrecked like a war-torn, embittered veteran. Amelie will always be my Somme, my Stalingrad, my Okinawa, my Saigon, my Gulf, my Afghanistan. A bullet embedded in my spinal cord with her name scratched into the grinning, bronze surface.

I'm an emotional and psychological gimp from this evening onwards.

Happy Fucking Birthday, you piece of shit.
A year from now, Amelie will die.

She's two hours late. I wait. I order another scotch and another. Then another.

Maybe it's at the time I'm on my seventh scotch or my fourth rum, or maybe it's when I'm falling down the weathered stone steps leading to the Thames on Victoria Embankment. Or maybe it's when I'm vomiting into the slime-colored water over the railings, Big Ben looming over me like a lighthouse for ghosts at the heart of London. The statue of Queen Boudicca damning me with eyes set in cracked stone.

Amelie stands me up on my birthday.

Amelie is fucking a guy she met on an internet chat room, in a cheap bed and breakfast a few blocks from where we're supposed to meet. I'll spend the rest of the night in a cell for a drunk and disorderly. Amelie will avoid me for a week, telling me she's still pissed off over the argument.

She'll finally tell me the truth a month later, over coffee in a Starbucks, but only after I've checked her mobile phone while she's in the restroom and find she's been sending nude photographs to the guy. Some skin-head prick named Michael from South London somewhere. Pictures of her tits and pussy. The backdrop to the photos: the shower in *my* apartment.

Terminal-stage cancer probably doesn't hurt as badly as these photographs do as I grit my teeth and force myself to look at them on the screen of her phone. She'll wail out a shocked and angry noise when she comes back to the table. Snatch the phone from my weak hands. People in the coffee shop will gasp, mumble to each other and stare.

I'll try to wrestle the phone back out of her grip to check for more. More wounds. More harms to inflict on myself. She'll hold it close to her chest, running out of the coffee shop and into the nearest underground station. I'll chase after her, shouting her name. Gawkers will gawp, gasping, tittering, and tutting. A guy giving out newspapers will knowingly grin and shake his head.

I'll finally find her at the far end of the platform, and she'll nonchalantly pass me the phone, telling me that if I don't trust her, if I'm that fucking paranoid, I can look at her phone, but it'll damage our relationship beyond repair. She doesn't know if she'll be able to forgive me. Trust me again. Somehow, suddenly, *I'm* the piece of shit. When I hold the mobile phone in my trembling hands, all the messages, pictures, and call logs will have been deleted. Erased. Everything. Amelie will just shrug and gaze at me with eyes deader than stagnant puddles. She'll slowly move in reverse, onto the next tube train and leave me standing there. Tears dribbling from my face. Hating myself more than I could ever hate her. Hating that falling in love with this woman made me this vulnerable, this weak, this addicted.

The announcement over the tube station speaker tells me on loop to "mind the gap."

Later, I'll ride the train too, hurtling, rattling around in pitch-black circles and figure-8 shapes for hours on end. Staring at my ghostly reflection in the dark mirrors of the windows across from me. A feeling like I'm rotting from the inside out spreading through my upper body.

In the following days, I'll drink myself into a coma. Amelie, discarded and alone herself, will blow up my phone with photographs of us together: happier days, smiling selfies, and holiday snaps. Then, when that doesn't work for her, pictures of shallow self-harms, she'll beg me back, using raw wrists and forearms with bloody gashes desecrating her body as some kind of negotiating collateral. This is how much she needs me, she'll tell me. I'll be moved. Tell myself that's how much she truly loves me. She'll come over. I'll let her in. She'll gaze over the clusters of empty and half-drunk bottles around my apartment and smile a little to herself but say nothing about it.

We'll talk it over; she'll tell me it was only the once. That guy, Michael, was the only one. It was a stupid mistake. She was drunk. He asked her if she wanted to "Netflix and chill," she'll say. She just went to his flat to watch some movies. He forced her. She was raped. It meant nothing. She would never do anything like that ever again. Blaming the abortion. She just wanted to stop the hurt inside herself, she'll say. She'll kiss me and gaze into my eyes and lie. I will become Samson. She'll hack off my hair.

I'll let her. I deserve it. And I don't want her to go. I'm a junkie. Junk sick. DTs. Without her, I'm beyond nauseous. Exhausted. Anxious. Agitated. Palsied and palpitating. I can't sleep. I can't eat. I am so far down, I no longer know which way is up. I just crave a fix. To feel somewhat normal again.

A few weeks will pass. We'll argue again. I'll throw her out of my apartment. She'll disappear into the night again. She'll send me photographs of fresh cuts she'll make with a pair of nail scissors on her wrists and thighs. Escalations. Proof of life. Proof of need. Proof of love.

I'll attempt to call her. Her phone will be dead. Switched off again. I'll try her so many times, I'll lose count. I stare into nothingness, watching nights become days.

This time, it'll be some guitar-playing rockstar wannabe she's fucking.

She'll come to my apartment a week later, in tears. Telling me she met him that first night we argued, when his band was playing at a bar in Soho and she'd gone to calm herself down. Telling me she only met him twice. Fucked him twice. Two nights only. In his Chelsea apartment. Tell me she was really drunk both times. Didn't want to do anything but he forced her. Raped again. She will say she doesn't know why she puts herself in those dangerous situations. Saying she's too sad. Too upset. The abortion. She can't recover from it.

She'll tell me she can't remember anything else and doesn't want to talk about it anymore because it hurts too much. She'll place her mobile phone screen-down. Take it everywhere with her. I'll catch her sending texts to the guy. Smiley face emoticons. I'll try to smash it against the wall. She'll lock herself in the bathroom and cut her thighs with a piece of broken glass. Screaming through the closed door that it's all my fault. I made her feel like a slut. I didn't help her. She didn't want to have the abortion. She wanted the baby.

Why was I punishing her so much? Why did I hate her so much? She only wanted forgiveness and love, she will wail. She'll blame me. She'll blame the termination. I'll blame myself, too. The black-and-white sonography picture of the baby will be waved in my face like a razor blade. I'll throw her out of my apartment again. The neighbors will complain. They'll threaten to call the police. Amelie will fade into the night once more. A shadow.

She will send me a text message three days later. I'll read the message, drunk with swollen eyes. She'll tell me she's checked at a clinic. She's got two doses of the clap. Syphilis. Gonorrhea. Fuck. My prick starts itching before I'm even through reading the message.

I'll drink what remains of a bottle of whiskey slumped on the kitchen floor. My back against the small refrigerator. A black dress Amelie left behind clasped to my face. Inhaling the lingering scents of her. The fabric on my fingers. Watching an ant scurry around in large loops on the worn linoleum. I'll vomit down the front of myself, the dress, and black out.

Days will pass.

There will be many phone calls but none of them from Amelie. I'll let the phone ring itself out of battery. Let it die with everything else.

I drag myself to the boxing gym, still drunk, and spar viciously. Dropping my hands. Biting down on the gum shield. Wanting one of the pros to knock me the fuck out. Split my face wide open. Leaning back into the ropes, swallowing blood until the coach wrenches me out of the ring and tells me to go home and get my fucking act together. Wanting to tell him I'm on the verge of the final round but say nothing. Swallowing words down with the bitter aftertaste of my own blood.

Weeks will pass.

I'll shuffle from kitchen to bed to toilet in a thick, black, moist fog. I forget. I scratch at myself and growl out imaginary conversations down bottles. My little savings are gone. The landlord keeps posting threats of eviction through my letterbox. I stop reading them after the fifth.

Amelie comes around. I know it shouldn't, but it feels like a reprieve. I let her in. She accuses me of throwing her away again. We argue. I drag her out of my apartment. Throw her purse into the street. She throws her high heels at the locked door. The neighbors thump on the walls and yell out of their chained doors. Amelie screams outside my building. I close the blinds and open a new bottle of bottom-shelf whiskey. I hear police radio chatter and people muttering outside my door. I crawl underneath blankets piled on the broken-down sofa and ignore the knocking and calling.

More weeks pass.

I drink less and try to eat more. I sober up. I go to work and beg my boss not to fire me. He doesn't. He loans me money. I pay my back rent. The landlord grumbles and thumbs the banknotes. Pats me on the back and tells me to get back out there and find the woman I deserve. A nice woman. I almost smile at that. Amelie is the woman I deserve.

Amelie calls. Amelie texts. I ignore her. I go no contact. My silence makes her more desperate. Her biggest fear is being alone with herself. This is the biggest sin I commit in her eyes.

I startle awake in the mornings with over a hundred missed calls on my mobile phone. Hand-scribbled notes crumple through the letterbox. She keeps coming back each time, murmuring confessions in drips and drops like a broken, trickling faucet. I know I'm only seeing the tip of the black iceberg of who she is now, but the more it hurts, the more I take her back. It's a vicious circle of pleasure and pain.

I am misery. Amelie is my company.

All of this sounds too fucked up to be believable. But Amelie was unbelievable.

She became a black hole, and she infected me with all that emptiness. I think that's love. Love is the beast that kills and devours everything it touches. Love makes us all into the best or worst versions of ourselves.

When we both finally calm down enough to talk sense, laying naked in my bed together, her long, blonde hair flowing over my chest, I ask her how she can tell me she loves me and then hurt me by cheating. She says it was only because she'd been depressed and angry. She had felt lonely and hollow since the abortion. We'd been arguing a lot. She was jealous of my happiness. She didn't know if I still wanted her. She thought I was planning to break up with her. She promises to go to therapy. I do, too. Neither of us will ever go.

And finally, in the end, I forgive her because she cries and pleads for that forgiveness.

But the truth is my life just hurts too much without her in it and the times when I'm with her feel too good. I *am* a crackhead for her. Unable to give her up, even though I know she will never really change, and neither will I. Amelie is the sickness I cannot ever fully recover from. I don't want to.

I tell myself I deserve to be hurt and I still do deserve it. I should've been a better man when it mattered the most.

Whatever we had, it died with the baby we killed and we became two hurt people hurting each other. Punishing each other. Tied together. Slowly stabbing each other to death in the dark with what we think is meant to be love.

I turn to look Katherine dead in the eyes. "Negative points? No, I don't think Amelie really had any. I love her despite everything. That's what love is supposed to be, isn't it? Acceptance? Forgiveness?"

"What do you think, Vincent?"

"I don't know," I say to the bird of paradise.

The joints in Katherine's chair screech again and then there's nothing but the hum of the air-conditioner, water rushing through a pipe somewhere in the walls, a car's brakes squealing far off and my own ragged breathing. "What do you think, Vincent?"

We're jostled by a crowd squeezing into the late-night tube. Amelie's gripping the collar of my leather jacket, pulling us closer together. Her smile radiating the whole train carriage. The lights of the underground dancing in her dark eyes. In my arms. Head against my chest. Arms moving up and around my neck. My hands around her waist. Her long hair tied up, giving off the sweet scent of a tangerine shampoo. I breathe it in. Deep. The rattle of the train passing over the tracks fades away.

"What do you think, Vincent?"

Morning sunlight pours through bedsheets. Underneath the covers with her. Unrestrained laughter. The colors of our flesh together juxtaposed pure white linen.

"What do you think, Vincent?"

The smell of antibacterial liquid, the whirring buzz of a tattoo needle. Amelie grinning at me from the leather chair as the tattooist etches the design that I chose for her into the flesh of her stomach. Matching tattoos. We hold eye contact the whole time as though we're fucking.

"What do you think, Vincent?"

The sounds of slow-moving water. Water caressing water—fingers softly on ivory piano keys. Amelie's moist skin in the golden heat of candlelight mixed with bathwater. Whispering to me to kiss her, hold her.

"What do you think, Vincent?"

St. Paul's Cathedral, her hands trailing the aged stones. A serenity flowing like unspoken things, mingling with the summer light pouring like bronze dust through brightly stained glass.

"What do you think, Vincent?"

Swaying together in the middle of a restaurant. The waiters have pushed a few tables aside. "Can't Help Falling in Love" plays from a record player on the far end of the bar. We have the whole place to ourselves. Dancing slowly together among the lacquered bamboo interior and potted plants.

"What do you think, Vincent?"

Rain falling from a pitch-black sky outside, torrential downpour, Hollywood-esque, raindrops catching the lights on the wet concrete like supernovas.

"What do you think, Vincent?"

Moving slowly against Amelie, underneath the orange glow of a streetlamp. Kissing her mouth. All I can taste is rain. I am full of rainwater. Standing motionless now. Her hands against my chest. Pushing. Her face turned away.

"What do you think, Vincent?"

"I don't know."

"Vincent…I…love you… It's over…I'm dead…"

"Let me see your face this last time, at least."

"I can't. Please go."

Bathed in a dark blue spotlight. Soaked through.

She's wet underneath my fingertips.

All I have is handfuls of rainwater.

She's not there.

I am full of rainwater.

She's gone now.

She's dead now.

The early hours of morning. Mourning.

My wristwatch stuck at 4:44.

Almost daylight. The nothing space in the middle of night and day. The deep blue of being in between things.

A migraine growing, pulsing, clotted in my brain. Lying in bed. The covers kicked down.

The miserable light of another day pouring through the dirty window. The whirring of traffic on a motorway far off. A siren somewhere.

My prick in my fist. Pulling and yanking images of Amelie from my memory. The way her naked body fit against my own. Her nipples underneath my teeth. Her lips, her mouth, her thighs holding me tightly inside her. The way she tasted. The way she smelled. Her lips on my closed eyelids.

Her breath on my face.

Her fingertips on my face.

The way she laughed with her eyes.

The way she loved me.

The way she doesn't love me now.

Everything is dead.

Dead. Dead. Dead.

She's dead.

Pushing the pillow over my face to stifle the sounds of my pathetic weeping and to soak up the snot seeping like rainwater from my nostrils.

The early morning hours will not cease. They're flooding into the room. The future doesn't stop its march onward, crushing the past underneath its heavy feet. Ocean waves. Unrelenting. A tsunami. I'm drowning.

I can't live.

I can't die.

I can't forget.

I can't even really remember.

I throw the pillow onto the floor and lie there, watching the birth of a day spreading across the cracked ceiling like a leaking abscess of the past.

What do you think, Vincent?

I think it is 4:44 in another aborted suicide morning.

FOURTEEN

"Hey, Vin! Do you want to see some of my paintings?" Beatrice talks fast, nervously, but grins cheekily. "I need an honest opinion on them. I know it sounds very stuck-up and cringe, but I've got to say I'm pretty disappointed by a lot of the people in this hellhole. No one knows fucking shit about art here, you know? Fucking plebs, the lot of them."

I catch myself automatically smiling at the chirpy and sarcastic sound of her voice. We've been eating together a lot recently. Every day. Breakfast. Lunch. Dinner. Tea and toast. Even taking our meds together. She stands outside the toilet door when I vomit sometimes. She doesn't like it, but she tries. She's been coming to my room a lot, too. For the first time in a long time, I have something to look forward to that exists outside the memories of Amelie I need to replay over and over in my head.

She's leaning through the doorway of my room. I can only see the top half of her body. The wrinkled, baggy Rolling Stones T-shirt she's always wearing. Her wild, dirty blonde hair hanging down like the unwatered, tangled leaves of a houseplant. A roll-up trailing smoke in her fingertips. Lips redder than usual. She's wearing mascara.

"I'm sorry to say that I'm just another fucking pleb, Beatrice. I don't know shit about art, either. Are you wearing makeup today or what?"

"Yeah, I am, actually. You noticed, huh? I'm happy."

"Sure. I think you look very pretty."

She blushes a little. Grips the rolled cigarette in between her teeth and poses with hands on her hips. The fresh color rising in her cheeks and throat makes her look more beautiful. Healthier. More alive.

There's a small stab of jealousy that splinters the back of my head like glass.

"Well, thank you, Vincent. What were you doing in here, anyway? Were you wanking? Pulling your pudding? Jerking off? You naughty, filthy little man!" she squeals, each question raising in volume and temper, then she lets out a breath after the crashing crescendo. Standing, squinting one eye closed to the smoke and slowly sucking on the cigarette while holding bemused eye contact.

It's my turn to blush. Feel my face burning up. I shake my head "no" in between nervous chuckles.

"You *actually were, weren't you*?!" She shrieks laughter.

"What? Wanking? Knocking one out? Jerking off? No, no, I wasn't. I haven't. Not recently. Not successfully, anyway."

"So, do you want to?"

"Jerk off?"

"No, arsehole. Do you wanna see some of my fucking paintings, or don't you?"

"Oh, right. Yeah, sure, I'd like that. Like I said, though, I'm not much of an art critic."

"Honesty is all I'm really looking for. Tell me if they're shit or not. You're pretty fucking honest, so it should be easy for you, no?"

"When you say I'm honest, do you mean I'm a socially retarded arsehole?"

"Those are *your* words, not *mine*, Vinnie." She pokes her tongue out at me like a little brat, and for a moment, I can imagine what she looked like as a child, before life grinded her into what she is today.

"I think you may be 'projecting,' little Katherine wannabe?"

"Fuck off," she coughs out a laugh with clouds of smoke.

I grin despite myself.

"If you're honest about the paintings, you may just get the hand job you obviously desperately need." She winks.

"Wow! A hand job from a mentally ill artist? Now, that's an offer I won't refuse. Come on then, you better show me these finger paintings you've been doing with your own feces," I say, nodding towards the corridor.

"Yeah, but one thing though, there's a clause. I didn't say *I* was the one who was going to give you the hand shandy."

"Don't say Katherine," I groan.

"No, I was going to get Bertie to wank you off."

We both spit out giggles. They fill the entirety of the tiny room like bright sunlight.

"On that note, let's just stop all this masturbation talk and go look at some crappy paintings," I say.

"Fuck off, they're not *that* bad. We'll have to hurry now because I'm going into town in a little bit." Beatrice picks up a sock from my floor and tosses it at me.

"Now, *you* can fuck right off! Going *out*? With whom?"

"Davina. You know, the little part-time nurse, she's taking me into town with her. Do you want anything while I'm out and about?"

"A bottle of whiskey and some acid would be nice. I did ask my parents, but they couldn't swing it, apparently. Squares."

"I was thinking more along the lines of smuggling you in some proper coffee."

"Well, if alcohol and psychedelic drugs are completely off the table, I guess I could make do with some Nescafé."

Beatrice sucks air through her teeth and faux grimaces. "Nescafé may be pushing your luck, mister."

"You tight-fisted cheapskate!"

"Oh, really? Tight-fisted? Now you're seriously only getting Tesco's own brand!"

"Did you ever think there would be a time in your life when you would be arguing about which granulated instant coffee to smuggle into a mental health clinic?"

"No, but I never imagined there would be a time where I tried to kill myself, either."

"Yeah, that's a fair point, I guess. Let me get dressed and I'll be right out." I get up slowly because my head's still groggy and fucked up from the morning meds. They've upped my dosage. I shake off the bathrobe and pull on a gray, baggy sweater over my shirt and a pair of black jogging bottoms over my shorts. Push the greasy, lank hair hanging in my eyes back over my head.

Beatrice is leaning against the wall, humming, and inspecting her chewed-up nails when I step into the corridor.

She looks beautiful, standing there in the sun. "*Wow*, you even got dressed-up for me," she says, glancing my body up and down, eyes wide, sarcastically shocked.

"Yeah, well, it's a special occasion, right? Your first exhibition and all that."

She takes my hand in hers, catching me by surprise and impatiently pulls me along the corridor towards the common room. Our rubber soles squeaking over the linoleum. Yellow bars of sunshine arranging themselves through windows. The weather warmer today. A lot of patients and staff cluster around, talking. Laughter bellows from the cafeteria. The atmosphere in the corridor is strange. I feel strange. Gravity doesn't feel as restrictive. The lights seem brighter, softer. My eyes don't sting. The joints connecting my bones move fluidly. I wonder if I might be happy again. I don't know.

Glancing out of a window into the courtyard, I see Bertie standing there. Grinning like an idiot savant at a butterfly in the palms of his open hands.

Amelie flashes through my mind.

I'm staring directly into the center of the burning sun.

I wrench my hand from Beatrice's, falling back a little. She skids to a stop. It feels as though I'm looking at her back for a long time. I can see the definition of her shoulder blades and each knot of her spinal cord through the dark cotton of her T-shirt. The silhouette of her bra clasp. She speaks over her shoulder, "You okay back there, Vincent?"

"Yeah, I'm fine. Why?"

"I don't know. Just checking, I guess." She shrugs.

The scent of Amelie's perfume on the air, on my clothes, my hands. "Can you smell perfume?"

"Vincent's phantom smells again," she sighs.

"Chanel? Can you smell it?"

"In this place? You're joking, right? You're imagining things again."

"No, forget it. Come and check this out, though." I lightly grip her elbow for balance and nod out the window, towards Bertie and the butterfly.

When she glances out there, her brown eyes dancing over the courtyard, Bertie and the butterfly disappear. "What? I can't see anything."

"Ah, it's nothing now. Something I thought I seen."

"I told you! Imaging things," she says, softly elbowing me in the ribs.

The common room is empty when we step inside. Stinking of chlorine, stale smoke, and ammonia. The television fixed to the wall left on. A cartoon, *Tom and Jerry*, plays with the sound on low. Beatrice stands, hesitating, chewing her thumbnail.

The canvasses lean against the far wall, underneath the window that overlooks the car park. Her paintings are very good. The more you look at them, the more beautiful they become, just like the painter. She's painted a lot of trees. Dead trees in hues of blue or on fire. There's a tree painted in thick white-and-black strokes like knife wounds. The last painting in the series is a cherry blossom tree in full blossom of pink and deep green tints.

Beatrice toes the canvas with a laceless Converse shoe and says, "That's my happy place, right there."

"I thought you said you didn't have one."

"I don't. Doesn't mean that I don't want one. Do you believe in reincarnation, Vincent?"

"What? Like you're born again when you die? Come back as some kid that's going to grow up to be a bank clerk or something?"

She shrugs. "Yeah, I guess so. But I don't wanna come back as a human. Fuck that. I wanna come back as a blossom on the branch of a cherry blossom tree. Be beautiful just for a singular moment and then gone on the wind. They've got cherry blossoms out in Japan. Saw a lot in Tokyo when I was out there. In the spring. They bloom for a couple of weeks and then spend the rest of their time in the gutter."

"You lived in Japan?"

"Yeah, years back, after university. I want to go back there one day, when I'm better. I'm going. Anyway, that's what I want in my next life. To be like those cherry blossoms."

"You want to be in the gutter? I've been there, Beatrice, and it isn't that great."

"Why not? Spend my afterlife the same way I spent this one. But at least, I'd be beautiful."

"You're beautiful now, Beatrice."

Her eyes flicker and the shadow of a smile shades the edges of her lips. She takes a few steps closer to me.

I can smell her. My face feels sunburnt. "So, what do the other trees represent?" I lean real close to the canvas in front of me. The bones in my back crack. "They supposed to represent your mental state now or what?"

"*Bing bing bing!* 100 points, Vin! I knew I wasn't making a mistake when I asked you and not Mark or Norman." She smirks. "So… What do you really think then? Don't be kind. Let me have it with both barrels."

"What do I think? I think they're fucking great." I twist my head away from the paintings to look her in the eyes. She may be smiling again, but I can't tell because she's holding her hands to her mouth as though she's whispering a secret.

When I was eight years old, I tried to hang myself.

"Are you fucking with me, Vincent?"

"No, seriously. I mean, they look real. Like photographs. The detail is really great. A lot of feeling is conveyed. To be honest, I was expecting pretty shitty stuff, but these are all excellent. Really excellent. You should be more confident in your talents."

"I guess I have my good days and my bad days with confidence, but I feel more confident than I did when I first got here. That's for fucking sure."

"Shit, how bad was life before?" I pick up one of the paintings and awkwardly walk around, searching for a hook or nail to hang it from.

"Bad enough to put me here. I don't have to tell you. You know that already, right? That's one of the things I like about you." She blushes. "As a *friend*, I mean."

There's not a single thing to hang the picture from so I carefully place it back down with the others.

"We *are* good friends now, aren't we, Vincent?"

"Sure, you're one of the only friends I've got. The only friend *I want*. At the moment." I wink.

Her face flushes again. An awkward silence falls on us like a fine dust coating everything. Words unsaid and words unheard for a long time like an unused room, the furniture covered with crisp, white sheets. Shadows slow dancing in derelict rooms. I pretend to look out the window at a crow perched on a telephone wire and change the subject back to her art. "Well, looking at your work now, you've definitely inspired me to try and start writing something again."

"A novel?"

"Yeah, maybe I'll try and write something about Amelie."

She smiles, but her eyes catch the yellow light of the day dully, like reflections of sun in puddles after a rain.

"I'm really happy you showed me, Beatrice."

"Really? In that case, I'm happy too. Thank you for your kindness, Vincent."

"I wasn't being kind. Just being my usual, honest self. You've got real talent."

"Maybe you'll let me read your stuff too," she says as she picks gray fluff from the shoulder of her T-shirt then crosses her arms around herself. "What kind of things did you used to write about? Before, I mean."

"I don't know. Angsty poems. Crap like that, mostly. I was working on a crime noir novel for a while, a long time ago. Gave it up like the bad habit it was."

"What, like one of those gum-shoe detective stories? Dickhead Tracy?"

"Yeah, shite like that, I guess." I laugh.

"Would you write something for me, Vincent?"

"For you? Like what?"

"A poem or some fucking thing like that. I don't know, but I really want to read it."

"A 'poem or some fucking thing like that'?"

"Yeah, I don't know, something like *violets are blue and so am I. These drugs make my cock flaccid, I want to die.*"

"Wow, that was Shakespearian! Anyway, who told you my cock was flaccid?"

"Oh, yeah, Katherine told me. We're always gossiping about your little, flaccid cock in my sessions. It's the main topic of our conversations, you know?"

"Small *and* flaccid?! That lying Canadian bitch promised me she'd keep all that a secret! It was only small and flaccid the one time, I swear to God!"

We both laugh, standing in front of each other like two old friends on a train platform. My face pleasurably aches. Moisture clouds my vision. Something akin to contentment bounces off the common room walls like a madman in a padded cell.

"Ah! That reminds me! Important question, Vincent." Beatrice beams. Rocking back and forth on her heels.

"Okay, shoot!"

She licks her lips. "Do you prefer full bushes, trimmed bushes, or waxed bushes?"

"Huh?!" I cough. Splutter. Laughing with my hands shoved deeply into the pockets of my jogging bottoms.

"I feel this is something I really need to know," Beatrice dead pans. Playing with the hem of her T-shirt. Pouting.

"Wow. That question really came out of nowhere, huh? Wasn't expecting *that. At all.*"

"Yeah." Her face shifts serious. She sighs, "I'm feeling so fucking rough and bored all the time and I have many big questions that need answering. Some of the most important questions, Vincent."

"Well, if it's important and you've really got to know. Trimmed or waxed, I guess. No one likes the 1970s porno look anymore."

"My pussy is like a dumpster fire in a jungle right now," she sighs again.

"1970s porno dumpster fire in the jungle?"

"I wish. More like 1870s. It's a rather Victorian dumpster fire," she finishes the sentence in a posh accent. Cleanly enunciating each word.

"Thanks for sharing that, Beatrice." I pull on the waistband of my bottoms, peering inside and pretending to examine my dick. "Yep, still totally flaccid, I'm afraid."

She doesn't seem to notice the joke and shrugs. "I'll get some waxing strips or something today. Waxing strips are allowed in here, you think?"

"In the ward? For the sake of your pussy, let's hope so!"

She glances at her wristwatch. The clouding on her face dissipates, and she finally smiles again. "I've got to go and meet Davina at the reception desk now, Vincent. But I promise to bring you back something cool from town, okay?"

"Yeah, even something Tesco's Own Brand would be appreciated." I nod.

As she passes me on her way out, she stops, seems to consider something, then leans in clumsily. She kisses me on the mouth. Her lips are hot. A light, flowery taste. Our tongues find their match and move slowly against each other's. Strangers brushing past each other on a train. I don't know how long we stand there like that, but she finally pulls away and skips out of the common room with her head down. She doesn't look back at me but, somehow, I know she's smiling. Maybe I know it because I'm smiling too.

Alone, I fall onto the sofa, forcing the dusty air to angrily hiss out of the cracked faux-leather cushions. I slouch there, picking yellow sponge from a tear in the arm and watching the television. Commercials play. I catch the scent of Chanel No. 5 again. Sniffing the air like a cocaine freak. It's as though Amelie is in the room with me. The two of us together again. Ghosts haunting each other in empty rooms.

Black and gray static burns up the flashing images on the television screen.

A pain behind my eyes like a day-old, red wine hangover.

On the screen, Amelie rushes into an old-fashioned kitchen decorated with blinding white lilies. Her parents are dressed up for a special occasion and setting a table for breakfast, while waitstaff wander around in the background, carrying bouquets and trays of food.

"Is that the time?" Amelie asks. She's wearing a pearl-colored bridal dress and has red hibiscus flowers tied-up in her long, peroxide-blonde hair. She looks even more beautiful than I remember. An ache like dry ice in my chest.

"Oh, your hair is lovely, dear," her mother says before being interrupted by the doorbell. "That'll be the bridesmaids," she says cheerfully.

"Come on, love. Look! I've even got your old favorites," Amelie's father says, bringing her over to the breakfast table and showing her a bright orange box of breakfast cereal. Her father is a reanimated corpse. He looks like the crypt keeper from *Tales from the Crypt*.

"Delicious flakes of corn, drenched in ice-cold milk. Cornflakes. How could you have forgotten how good they taste?" Amelie says softly in the voiceover.

"Vincent's really got a lot to live up to, Daddy," Amelie speaks into the camera, and my eyes widen as she slides a spoon of cereal into her full-lipped, rose-red mouth.

"Too good to be forgotten. Have you forgotten, Vincent? Please, don't forget me, Vincent! Don't forget! I don't want to move on! I love you! Me! *Me*!" the hysterical voiceover version of Amelie screams. The speakers on the television vibrate, crackle. The screen cuts to black with a gray bubble in the middle. The bubble pulses and jerks. The sound of a muffled heartbeat pumps out from the walls.

I'm staring at an ultrasound on the television now.

The ultrasound.

Our ultrasound.

I sit up and twist my head around the room. Stand up shakily. Pins and needs puncture my feet. I stumble over to the television, jabbing at the buttons. Each channel is the same pulsing image. The beating of the heart grows louder. Up through the floorboards. Ripping through the walls. Tearing apart the insides of my skull.

I squeeze my palms into my ears until my head aches, but the sound doesn't diminish. I stagger and fall out of the common room, sliding along the corridor wall until I'm back in my room, spreading photographs of Amelie across the bedsheets, the folded suicide letter crumpled in my palsied hands.

I can't forget. I won't forget.

I don't want to forget.

I don't want to move on.

The setting sun colors us in a taint of house arson orange.

Amelie's brown eyes flicker over me. Brassy. Constant. November bonfires dying down. Ash on the wind and in my mouth. A vibrancy on the early evening air as though we are about to fuck or fight. Our two favorite pastimes. Highly skilled and competitive at both.

She's lazily moving her arms, treading water. Skin creamy white and cold, cutting through the blurry ocean surf. "I can't stop thinking about it, Vincent." Seawater running in rivers down her cheeks, collecting on her jaw like raindrops on a windowsill.

"It makes me feel hollow. When I wake up in the morning, I can feel it. The emptiness. I can feel it growing where the baby should have been. It was a mistake. We made a mistake. I want to go back, but I can't now. It's too late."

"I know," I say. I'm holding her letter. It's turning into a pulpy mess from the ocean water

"Will we have another baby, Vincent? Can we?"

I look at her. Looking out of the window in my room. At the sky above the car park. I don't say anything because I didn't answer her that day in Margate. The question went unanswered because I didn't want to answer it. Didn't want her to know the answer. I knew, I know, I was losing her then.

We stay in the tide, shivering. I don't know how long we've been looking at each other like this. Treading water together. Here in the North Atlantic Ocean. The surf coming harshly, rocking us back and forth like dead things hanging from the bottom of ropes. Sounding like a storm pouring through my arteries.

She is dead.

I am dying.

"Is this the afterlife, Amelie? Are we blossoms gone in the wind?" I whisper, holding my hand up into the air, seawater falling like rain from my fingertips.

She laughs. That dopamine sound always squeezes my heart in its small, scarred fists. Snatches at my breath like a blade running through unforgiving skin. I try to move closer, but, with every motion I make, she pushes herself away. I can't breathe. My fingers struggle with a cotton cord wrapped around my throat. I want her to stay. I want to stay. Here. In this place. With Amelie. Infinitely. All I need. All I want.

"It's getting cold, Vincent. Let's go back to the motel, okay?"

"No, stay a little longer." I splash at her. I remember this moment well. The day at the beach. One of our good times. Our better times. Standing in the ocean, we could almost forget the sins and crimes we committed on each other.

"I'm really cold, Vincent. Please? I don't feel like swimming. I just wanna go back and sleep."

I hold her close, wrapping my arms around her, pulling her into me—the same way I did back then. She's trembling. Her bikini top lime-green. I rub at my stinging eyes and it's orange, then brown. I blink and it's back to green. Everything is changing. I never change. I am the one consistency.

I hold her closer. Her tits heavy against my chest. We have no heartbeats because we are both dead and this is our reincarnated afterlife. We are cherry blossoms in the gutter and then gone.

We are dead.

We are shadows fading away in derelict rooms.

Something vicious moves in the surf. Ancient and pale green. Orange eyes burning. November fires. Medical scalpel teeth beaming through the water.

Amelie is gone.

This isn't a memory or a dream, nor is it déjà vu.

I open my mouth.

I cough up blood. Rose petals floating on the surf.

Love is an incurable, inoperable terminal illness, and I am dying from it.

I am dead.

She is gone.

FIFTEEN

"Surprise, Vincent!"

A small, thin, seemingly insignificant piece of white plastic with a blue line completely alters your life. Triggering an avalanche of choices, consequences, and regrets. Death.

Deaths.

Standing with my back against the crumbling brick wall of the supermarket around the corner from my apartment, Amelie is brandishing the third pregnancy test she's taken today up in the air between us. Almost triumphantly. A serrated blade. Her face and eyes the most radiant I've ever seen them. She's beaming pure white enamel. The smile of a woman who just found out she's going to be a mother. It's a moment that will define and mold her whole life.

My life, too.

Its decline and ultimate downfall.

I feel motion sick. Fight or flight chemicals flood my body. Mouth tasting of cigarette ash and last night's whiskey and vomit. A self-immolation of cold sweat burning me alive.

Media, television, movies—everything I've ever seen or watched has taught me to take Amelie in my arms, kiss her deeply and then jump around excitedly. *I am going to be a father. Something to be celebrated.*

Déjà vu.

I don't want to do any of that. I can't do any of that. All I want to do is vomit.

I just remain there, leaning against the supermarket exterior, glaring at that small piece of plastic in her hand that has changed everything in the seconds it took the chemical reaction to change the colors and make lines where there weren't any lines before. The word "fuck!" wrapped in barbwire and pulsing like a migraine in my brain.

"Vincent? Did you hear what I said? That's the third test that's positive now. Oh my god, I'm actually pregnant, Vincent. I'm really pregnant. What a surprise, huh!"

"Yeah, sure, it's definitely a surprise. You told me you were on the pill, so it's pretty much a pretty big fucking surprise for me."

"I *was* on the pill. I mean, I *am*."

"So, how the hell are you pregnant then?"

"I don't know. It just happens like that sometimes, I suppose. Aren't you happy? Excited, Vincent?" She holds out her hands, palms down to the cracked concrete. "Oh, my god. Look! I'm so excited, I'm shaking."

"No, it doesn't *just happen like that*."

"Well, I don't know. What do you want me to say?"

"There's nothing you can say now, I guess. But I think it's best not to get too happy or excited about it until we weigh up all of *our* options. Really given it some thought. Together."

"What do you mean? *Weigh up all our options? Give it some thought?* It's a baby, not a fucking holiday destination or a takeaway menu."

"I mean, I thought we already talked about this, Amelie. I told you I didn't want a baby right now."

"But I'm already pregnant, Vincent. It's done. Plus, you helped too, right? I didn't make a baby on my own. You chose not to wear a condom. You chose to come inside me."

"Because you said you were on the *pill*."

"I *am*! But I'm still pregnant."

"Fuck! Fuck! Fuck!"

A couple ugly teenagers gawk at us and giggle from a bus stop across the street.

They give me something to direct my anger towards. "Get the fuck out of here, you little cunts."

Amelie gasps, a hand pressed to her mouth. "Vincent, why are you behaving this way?"

My mobile screams into the moment. I yank it from my pocket, switch it to silent mode and slip it back in my pocket.

"Who was that?"

"Work. Probably trying to find out where I am."

"Liar! It was *her*, wasn't it?!"

"I said it was work and it *was* work."

"You should call them back then. Your boss is going to be angry again."

"No. Fuck it. I'm not exactly in the mood to be talking to anyone right now."

"What do you mean?"

"I can't help but think you did this on purpose."

"What's that supposed to mean?"

"You got pregnant on purpose."

"Why would I do that?"

"You know why!"

"No. No. No, I didn't do it on purpose. Vincent, I'm *having* this baby. I *want* this baby."

"I'm sorry. I just need time to think. I'm going to go home alone. I'll talk to you later."

"I can't believe you're acting this way, Vin!"

"Acting like what?"

"So cold and moody."

"I can't believe you're acting the way *you* are. This affects *both* of our lives. It's not just about what *you* want all the time. I need time to compute it all. My brain is going a hundred fucking miles a minute here."

"You're being really unkind and selfish, right now. I thought we would celebrate, at least," she pouts.

"Celebrate? Are you fucking crazy or what? We aren't even sure if we are having the baby or not, but you want to celebrate? You're the one being a selfish bitch about all of this."

"No, you're being so *selfish* and *horrible*, Vincent! I'm feeling really hurt."

"Wake up and smell the fucking coffee, Amelie. Every time we talked about it, I told you I didn't want a kid. Told you a hundred fucking times! Why the fuck would I celebrate?"

"Because you said we're serious. You said you love me."

"And I do. I'm sorry. Look, I've got to go. I want to think about this, and you really need to tell your mum. She's been a single mother too. I'm not going to marry you, so what's she going to think about that? Her daughter a single mother, as well."

"Oh my god! You selfish fucking piece of shit, Vincent! I can't believe you at all! I left my husband for you! Broke my marriage for you!"

"Don't talk like you were the only one, Amelie."

"Fuck you, Vincent! I knew it! This is because of her, isn't it? Your fucking ex!" She throws the pregnancy stick at me and it hits between my eyes and bounces onto the hot concrete.

The kids across the street cackle louder. Tears swell in Amelie's eyes. Her bottom lip trembles. I walk away before she can. A meter or so down the street, I glance over my shoulder and watch her bending down to pick up the pregnancy test from the pavement and slip it into her handbag. It's a pathetic looking gesture that creates a gnawing, frigid sensation to seep into my guts, my fingertips, then finally settles behind my eyes. I don't know a lot, but I know Amelie is right. I *am* a selfish, horrible, worthless piece of shit. But that's why I don't want a child right now. I feel bitter, as though I've been tricked. All of the times that she told me she was on the pill, I wonder if that was just another one of her lies. Or another one of the lies I told myself.

No.

Stop.

Go back.

"Surprise, Vincent!"

A small, thin, seemingly insignificant piece of white plastic with a blue line on it completely alters life. Triggering an avalanche of choices, consequences, and regrets. Death.

Deaths.

No.

Stop.

Go back.

Start again.

I can change it. Save her life. Our unborn child's. Maybe even my own.

I replay the memory over and over in my mind. Changing words. Altering facial expressions. Body language. Making it all different. In this version of the past, there's champagne splashed on concrete, shared from the bottle. Alcohol-flavored kisses. Laughter. The kids across the street cheer for us. *Congratulations.* I pull Amelie into my arms and lift her into the air. Her giggles climb the brick walls into the baby blue sky and into forever. Infinity.

When I open my eyes, it's dark. I'm in my room, there's still chicken wire in the glass of the windows. Someone is still yelling from somewhere down the corridor. Everything that mattered is still dead.

"Surprise, Vincent!"

Surprise.

SIXTEEN

"Surprise, Vincent!" Beatrice bursts into my room, swinging a white, plastic supermarket bag around her fist.

I startle, bashing the back of my skull on the wall. It makes a hollow cracking sound. I'm not surprised by the noise. I *am* hollow. Eaten from the inside out by my fucking feelings.

My head swims. I look to where Beatrice is standing, but my focus swings back and forth. Her silhouette is blurred. Unfocused. A pale, faded wraith hovering in an empty doorway.

She makes a croaked, gasping noise with hands clasped in front of her throat, the bag hanging from her featureless face—an obscene growth.

"Hey, sorry I made you jump. Maybe I should've knocked first."

I push my palms into my eye sockets. Holding them there. I don't want to see the stale reality of things today. I want the world to be blinded.

There's the ruffle of fabric and plastic as she makes her way further into my room, her weight pushing down, beside me on the bed. The mattress creaks and groans. The crook of an arm soft and wisp-like around my shoulders. "Vin, you okay? What's wrong?"

"Nothing. It's nothing. I'm fine," I spit out.

"Really? You can talk to me if you want to, you know?" She rubs the back of my head, where I struck the wall.

For a moment, I'm in a doctor's waiting room, watching a little blonde girl tear strands of her hair out.

"Yeah, I know. I said, it's nothing. There's nothing to talk about."

"You'll never get a blow job in this place if people see you crying like a little pussy all the time, Vincent."

I fight it, but the smile pushes its way into my cheeks, slicing through the fists still shoved into my eyes as though I'm an eight-year-old kid playing hide and seek.

1, 2, 3, 4, 5, 6, 7, 8, 9, 10. Ready or not, here I come.

"That's good because I wasn't crying. I have another migraine."

"I was only joking, but yeah, sure, a migraine makes your eyes leak sadness, right? Don't worry, I'd still blow you. *Only* out of pity though, of course."

I can hear the good-natured smirk in the waves of her voice. There's a long silence and then she whispers, "Oh, is this her? Amelie?"

I open my eyes to see a snapshot of Amelie held lightly in Beatrice's fingers. The photograph looks alien in another's hand. Someone else's history. Someone else's memory.

"Yeah, that's her. That's Amelie."

"She *is* really pretty, huh?" Beatrice says running the pad of her thumb over the smiling face of my traumatic Kodak nostalgia.

"Yeah, I know. I know. And I fucked it all up."

"Takes two people to fuck up any kind of relationship, Vincent." She shrugs, tossing the snapshot back on the bedcover, as though it's a creased magazine in a waiting room she's bored of.

I snatch it up and shuffle it back into the pile. "She's dead," I say too loud.

She tilts her head, gazing at my face for a long time. Her pupils flickering, flashing to take in each of my features carefully. Studying me. "Yeah, so you keep telling everyone… Look, come on. Come with me. I've got some presents for you that should help cheer you up right about now! Come on, move it, mister!" She roughly takes my hand in hers and pulls me up from the bed, exaggeratedly groaning at the weight. Wincing and clutching at her back as I make no effort to stand. Dead weight. "*Come on*, I said! Shake it, fat-boy. Let's go and get your presents, huh?" She gets me to my feet and pulls me stumbling after her, out of my room and back towards the common room.

The light moves over the freshly mopped floor like rainwater shining on pavements. I remember the television, the cornflakes commercial, and my mouth goes dry. An icy sweat dribbles down my spine. Heart beats like a dog barking in the night. Another panic attack claws at my door. Haven't had one in a while, but that black mutt is never far away. Always skulking around.

"Almost there, Vincent. You're going to love it. But you've got to be quiet, okay?"

I don't say anything as she pulls me into the common room, beaming, all mouth, lips, and electric eyes.

She slams the door shut, and we both stand, heavy breathing, leaning with our shoulders against it. There's heat thickly drifting off Beatrice, like wet concrete in a midday July sun. The common room is deserted as particles of dust drift and catch what little light seeps into the building.

"Most of the staff are watching the Arsenal game in the office, so we have a little time and a little privacy. Here are your first presents." She grins really wide, handing me the plastic supermarket bag. Inside is a packet of semi-crushed chocolate digestive biscuits, a carton of cigarettes, and a music magazine with a black-and-white Elvis cover.

I can't help falling in love with you.

I hold the gifts in my hands for a long time, staring down at them. I try to remember a time when someone did something this kind for me who wasn't related by blood. "Wow! I don't know what to say. These are great, Beatrice. Really, really great. Thank you. You shouldn't have spent your money on me though."

"Don't say that! I did it because I wanted to. I'm sorry there's no coffee, but I got something so *much* fucking better." She lifts the hem of her T-shirt and twists her hips to show me the plastic pint of whiskey pressed against her milky flesh, tucked into the waistband of her jeans next to her naval and what looks like a CD.

"Is that Jack Daniel's and Roy Orbison stuffed into your Levi's, Beatrice?"

"Yep, I love them both and they love me. It's an uncomplicated threesome that always makes me very horny."

We snort at the same time. She winks. My migraine seems to dissipate.

"How the hell did you afford all this stuff?"

She yanks the bottle and CD free from her waistband and triumphantly waves them in the air. Grinning. "I had some points saved up on my five-finger discount card. Besides, I never could resist the charms of Roy Orbison's greatest fucking hits."

"The whiskey though, the staff will go crazy when they find it."

She peels the plastic seal away from the top of the whiskey like she's unwrapping a condom. "They're not going to

find it, Vincent. It's only a pint and we're going to drink it fast."
She shrugs. "*And* I've got something that should buy us a little
more time and privacy."

"Yeah, what?" I say, glancing out the door window and
down the empty hall.

"*Ta-da!*" Beatrice says, pulling a large ring of keys from
the back of her stonewashed 501s. She jangles them in front of
my face, hypnotizing me for a few seconds.

"You stole the fucking keys, Beatrice?!" I hiss.

"*Davina's* set of fucking keys to be precise," she hisses
back, slowly sliding the key into the door while holding eye
contact. The locking mechanism clinks and clunks. "Now we are
locked up tight. Just you and me."

"What's the point in locking it? All the staff have keys.
If they find it locked, they'll just unlock it, anyway."

She gives me a trademark *I couldn't give a shit* shrug. "True,
it won't stop the staff coming in, but it'll stop the other nut
jobs—our esteemed peers—from wandering in and out and
fucking up the mood, won't it? Now stop making things
complicated, you party-pooping pussy, and go get the CD player
over there. I want to sing 'Pretty Woman' while we drink."

We grab the cushions from the sofa and toss them in the corner.
We sit on them, out of view of the long rectangular window in
the common room's door, passing the whiskey bottle back and
forth. Each taking long gulps of the amber liquid, setting our
chests on pleasant fire. Committing arson in our hearts. Our
shoulders and thighs pressing together. Beatrice singing along to
Orbison, her words mere whispers. She stops, leans forward to
turn down the volume, and looks at me thoughtfully for a long
time. Tilting her head and leaning into me. I think we're about
to kiss again, but a question leaves her lips instead. "Do you
think you're scared of the things you're scared of because,
subconsciously, you know they'll be the death of you? Like, if
you're terrified of horses. Does it mean you're going to be
trampled by one on a random Wednesday morning?"

"I don't know."

"Oh, just fuck off, will you?"

"What? What did I say?"

"The same thing you always say to my questions. '*I don't
know.*' It's rather infuriating, you know that?"

"Maybe it's because you always ask a lot of fucking weird questions. You ever think of that?"

"*Hey*! My questions are not fucking weird."

"They're not? You're asking if I think someone is scared of clowns because they know, somewhere deep down in their subconscious, they're going to be murdered by a clown one day? That's a weird fucking question, Beatrice."

We stare at each other. Solemn-faced, trembling, holding the laughter inside our stomachs like holding off a shuddering orgasm until we can't anymore, and Beatrice sprays whiskey through her lips and I spit a bourbon-flavored chuckle onto the threadbare floor. There are tears in our eyes, the kind you don't try to wipe away quickly. The kind of tears you let remain on your face until they dry, leaving salty stains behind.

Beatrice stands up to peer out the window, still grinning. "The coast is still clear. None of the fuckers heard. You know what I'm scared of?"

"Clowns with carving knives?"

"That's an easy thing to fear because it's not realistic, Vincent. Guess again."

"A swear jar and each time you say the word 'fuck,' you have to pay a quid?"

"Fuck off! I don't say the word 'fuck' *that* fucking much."

"Okay, so tell me what you're scared of, Beatrice."

"Promise that you won't laugh or anything?"

"I can promise that I'll *try* not to laugh, but that's the best I can do at this moment in time." I take a gulp from the whiskey and raise the bottle.

Beatrice pulls it from me, takes a mouthful and gargles before swallowing. Sucking in a deep breath, holds it and breathes out.

I feel it warm on my face like a July breeze.

"Okay, I'm ready. I'm ready to share with you, Vincent. But you better not laugh. I'm always scared of not being good enough. Not enough. Like, no one will ever accept me for me, for who I am. People always leave me. Yeah, I'm fucked up, but I'm a good person. Why isn't that ever fucking good enough? I'm so tired of being fucked over and thrown away like I'm trash. It's been the same since I was a fucking child and I'm so fucking sick of not being good enough."

"You're more than good enough, Beatrice," I say, softly placing my hand against her liquor-flushed cheek, cupping her chin in the palm of my hand. There are tears at the corners of her eyes again. "Thinking otherwise is just, well, fucking mental."

"Ah, and therein lies the problem," she says, pointing the neck of the bottle around the common room to emphasis the fact we're in a mental hospital, mental clinic, nuthouse, limbo, whatever.

Still holding her face in my hand. She pushes against it. Passes me the bottle. I drink. I shake the remnants and watch the way the light flows through the light brown liquid.

"You're one of the best people I've met, Beatrice."

"In this place?! That's hardly a fucking compliment, Vincent."

"Anywhere. Recently, because of you, I've been feeling a little better. I think you're great and you're good enough for anyone."

"I hope so," she murmurs. Trying to smile. I feel it falter against my palm. Shuddering, like a butterfly attempting to fly with a torn wing.

"I know so," I say, taking my hand away from her face and passing her back the bottle. "You need to drink more, Beatrice."

It could be 10 minutes or an hour later when the bottle is laid dead between us and the gunshot drumroll of Orbison's "Crying" starts spilling into the room in all its marvelousness.

"God, I fucking *love* this song *so fucking much*," Beatrice slurs a little, struggling to her feet and pulling me up after. "Dance with me, Vincent. Please."

"I think I'm too pissed to dance, even if I wanted to."

"Are you serious? On half a fucking pint?! You lightweight!" She giggles tipsily, shoving me hard back down onto the pillows. The pillows hiss exasperations of dust.

She stands over me, hands on hips. Pulls her hair free from a band, letting it wildly flow down her shoulders like rainfall. "Then I'll dance, and you watch me, okay?"

I can't say anything.

Beatrice does dance and I do watch.

I watch her moving like hot, flowing water. Pushing and rolling and bucking and swaying her hips to the beat of the song. I watch her running her hands over her body so damned slowly. Her lips mouthing the song's words without a single sound escaping them, but the sound of her breath quickens with the melody. The way the fabric of her T-shirt ripples, tightens over her breasts and stomach. The rosy, speckled rash at her throat. She pushes her fists into her eyes, twisting them, mimicking a childlike mourning and then slowly brings her arm into the air to point towards me.

There's a feeling boiling in me that isn't the whiskey. I haven't felt it since the last time Amelie and I were happy. Before sex became a serrated weapon or a test or a submission or an act of domination.

My heart hammering in beat with the song's drums.

Beatrice moving closer and closer. The song reaches its climax. By the time it takes me to blink, she's standing so close, I can smell her. The scent of a woman, mixed with bourbon, tobacco, and the soap she used in the morning.

The song finishes. The only sounds remaining are the rushed and shuddering, rhythmic waves of our breathing.

And then I'm pulling her down onto me and she's pulling my face into hers. The kisses come hard and fast. We bite and bump teeth. Clumsy, desperate, starving acts of war against our own unhappiness and insecurities. White flags. Surrender. Reprieve. Stays of execution. She pulls her mouth and hands away from mine, lifting the T-shirt above her head and unclasping the pink lace bra to unveil the milk-white breasts hidden beneath. Lifting my mouth to the hard nipple the same color as the lipstick smudged around her lips. Her breath hot on my head. "We can fix each other, Vincent. We can. We can. We can. Fix each other."

I bring her wrist to my lips and trace the pink, smooth scars there with my tongue. "I want to," I breathe. "I really wish I could."

We stop only to pull off her jeans and then she's easing down on me again, guiding me into her. Engulfing me into the deepest, warmest darkness of her.

Her mouth on mine again.

Her hair wrapped, twisted around my fingertips.

I kiss her tits and her neck as she moves in rhythm with me and against me. Say the words I've wanted to say for so long.

"I love you."

She holds my face in her hands as she moves her hips down slower, harder, taking me deeper inside her, gazing into my face as she murmurs the words I've wanted to hear for so damned long. "I love you, too, Vincent. I love you, too."

I kiss her mouth. Hold her tighter to me.

Amelie.

You are not dead.

I am alive.

SEVENTEEN

I can hear the ocean. Waves. A heartbeat.

We're in a motel somewhere.

Amelie and me.

Margate or Hanoi or Liverpool or Manchester.

London. We are in London.

Her head on my chest. Hand on my beating heart. Hair spilling over me like liquid fire.

She unwinds herself from my arms to rummage around the pockets of her jeans crumpled next to us. She sighs, humming a tune I don't recognize. Pulls out a packet of Golden Virginia tobacco and a pack of papers.

"Since when did you start smoking roll-ups?" I ask, pushing myself up on an elbow. The floor suddenly ice-cold. The pillows itchy.

"What? I've been smoking these since I was like 15. Is that what you mean?" She tilts her head, sticking her tongue out of the corner of her mouth as she frowns slightly, concentrating, carefully sprinkling the tobacco onto the brown liquorish paper.

"No, I mean you didn't smoke before."

"Huh? You see me smoking every day. All the time. Are you all right, Vincent?" She passes me the roll-up, our fingers touch. Beatrice smiles. The smile is shy and vulnerable.

"I'm okay, Am… Beatrice."

She flinches as though I've struck her. Deep lines like scars deepen in the pale flesh of her forehead and crinkle the skin around her eyes.

We aren't who I thought we were.

Not where I thought we were.

We are Beatrice and Vincent.

We're in the common room.

We are in Limbo.

Beatrice inhales the cigarette once and then snuffs it out hard on the CD case, tossing the dead butt underneath the billiard table.

Gravity pushes its filthy weight down on me. I repeat her name to convince myself. "Beatrice…"

She flinches again, but less this time. Chewing at her nail, her eyes very wet, oil-slick black ink spots fixed on the small block of deep, baby blue sky visible from the large windows overlooking the car park and a single dying tree. On one of the lower branches, a crow wears the color of a funeral and tears something apart between beak and claw.

Neither of us speaks for a long time. I can hear the pipes in the walls. A bulb in the ceiling. *Click, clink, clink.* Light. Darkness. Light. Darkness. My stomach whines and groans. Beatrice exhales deeply.

The sounds of the other patients, their problems, their sicknesses finally drift back down the hallway and through the walls and the locked door. Another metallic *click* from the radiator beneath the window. Beatrice stares and stares, gnawing her fingernail raw, somewhere else entirely. Somewhere far away. Plummeting through time and space within her own shadow-infested mind.

Softly, she clears her throat and then speaks without taking her eyes from the window. "I thought you lov— I thought you liked *me*, Vincent."

I clear my throat too, focusing on the side of Beatrice's face. Smooth. Marble white. She reminds me of the statues in museums. Ethereal, out of place and melancholic. "I *do* like you." I place my hand on her bare shoulder.

Her skin is fever hot. She flinches from my touch like a stray dog that's been kicked in the ribs too many times. It makes me want to take her in my arms and hold her until she's okay again. But I don't. I fold my arms tightly across my chest and glare at the room's warped, ghostlike image reflected at me from the darkened television screen on the opposite wall.

"You bullshit and lie to everyone, Vincent. Even yourself. But, please, don't do that to me." She snatches up her T-shirt, clumsily pulling it over her head. Shuffles back into her jeans from the position she's been sitting in. Her back to me still.

"What do you want me to say, Beatrice?"

"I don't know! How about the fucking truth for once, Vincent?"

"You know I'm in love with Amelie. You've known that all along. From day one."

"Fuck! You really do refuse to get better, don't you?"

"It's just the way I feel."

"So, what was that? Just now, with me? A little quickie in the nut house?"

"You wanted that just as much as I did."

"Yeah, but you know what the fucking difference is, Vincent? It actually meant something to me, you fucking oblivious idiot."

"I'm sorry, Beatrice, but I'm in love with Amelie. That's the obvious thing, isn't it?"

"Oh yeah, the dead girl. How fucking convenient for you."

"What the fuck are you talking about?"

"Her being dead. Pretty fucking convenient for you, isn't it? What a joke."

"Shut the fuck up. You have no idea what you're talking about."

"God, I almost feel sorry for you because you're not just manically depressed, you're truly fucking deluded. You're worse than Bertie, even."

"Fuck you, Beatrice."

"No, fuck you, Vincent! Amelie isn't even really fucking dead, is she? She's not here because she doesn't want to be. She didn't want you, Vincent! People break up all the time. Every fucking day. People get cheated on. People get fucked over. You know what? It hurts. It hurts *a lot* for a while. Sometimes for a long time. But guess what? People fucking get over it. So why don't you wake up, smell the coffee, and get the fuck over it finally, Vincent."

I shake uncontrollably. Blood viciously pulsing in my brain. "Yeah? Well, maybe you should take your own advice, Beatrice."

"What the fuck that's supposed to mean?"

"It means maybe I just wanted to get laid. Maybe I used you. Fucked you over? That's what you said, wasn't it? So just get over it too, Beatrice. Get over it!"

"I knew you lied a lot, but you really played me for a fool. Now, I know how Amelie must've felt."

"Get the fuck out of here and leave me the fuck alone, you dumb cunt."

"I feel so bad for you, Vincent."

"Don't feel bad for me. You're the one that got rejected *again*, Sylvia fucking Plath."

She gasps. The atmosphere becomes a vacuum. The hurt in her eyes seems almost infinite.

I've seen eyes like that before. Amelie. I hurt everyone I love, in the end.

I watch her stumble away. Punch drunk from my acidic words. I know she's right and I hate her for that. I hate myself more. She slams the door hard enough to rattle the windows. I'm not a good person. I am a piece of shit. I want to tell her that I'm sorry. I just can't control my feelings sometimes, and it makes me say awful shit to the people I love, so they'll hate me just as much as I hate myself. It's easier to kill yourself when you can feel like no one loves you. It is another lie you tell yourself. Another pill you have to swallow.

I want to cry, but I can't. When I open my mouth, I yell. I beat my fists on the floor. Screaming the word "FUCK" over and over again, until people in coveralls come into the room like rainwater flooding down a street in a storm.

EIGHTEEN

I don't leave my room. Days change the coloring on the wall. Someone, Beatrice, I guess, slips folded pieces of paper underneath my door. Letters. I don't know what they say. I leave them where they lay. I don't want to read them. Refuse to read them. Refuse everything.

I refuse my meds. I refuse the food. I refuse to talk. I refuse visits. A self-induced coma. I'm too sick. In the head. In the gut. In the fucking heart. I'm hollow. Already dead. I'm rotting. I feel my own degradation. My own decomposition.

Trying to remember Amelie's face, but nothing comes. Just a featureless store mannequin, stuck, unmoving in my mind. When I close my eyes, there's nothing there but white noise.

I keep them closed tight until my head pounds. Lost in my nothing. The cliffs. Attempting to reach Amelie there. Black scribbled on crumpled white paper. Warm rainwater in the palms of my hands.

It's only when I open my eyes that I notice my nosebleed. Blood on my hands.

Katherine tap, tap, tapping on my door. Pushing her way into my room with one of the other staff. Yammering on about meetings, interventions. I tune back out of her frequency. Wipe dribble from my face and go back to staring out of the window.

Refuse.

My parents knock, knock, knocking, on my consciousness hissing about treatments, interventions.

I refuse.

Beatrice whispering she's sorry, she's sorry, she's sorry. I stare at her until she leaves. She's a ghost.

How can we fix each other when we can't even fix ourselves?

I refuse. I refuse. I refuse.

My head aches, swelling, full of blood and jarred images like pieces of broken mirror scattered in my skull.

The word "intervention" pouncing around the room, an animal with claws drenched in gasoline, set on fire. Howling. Screeching.

I'm so fucking tired, I can barely breathe.

I give in. I give up. I tip all the little plastic cups of pills to my lips and swallow them.

Time passes.

When they come to take me, I let them.

NINETEEN

The sky is always the same deep shade of baby blue here.

Margate City.

With Amelie.

The clouds static. Unmoving. The ocean waves too loud. The only sounds I hear.

She's standing at the edge of the cliffs, drowned in the shadow of the lighthouse. Her back to me. Peroxide-blonde hair and lime-green dress catching in the wind. The fabric dancing twisted. Crumpled white paper in my palsied hands.

I call out her name. It echoes on forever.

She doesn't look back.

This is where she jumps.

This is where she leaves me.

This is where she dies.

My love.

The most beautiful things in this life are always the things full of death.

The people we love the most in this life are always the ones who kill us quickest.

I call out her name again.

"Vincent, I'm sorry, but it really is time now. You need to see this and start to accept it. Do you understand? I've been attempting to treat you with the usual methods of cognitive behavioral therapy, but recently you've become despondent. So, today, with your family's help, we're going to try a kind of drastic aversion therapy, okay? That means showing you what you've been avoiding. Forcing you to confront that which you deny. We need you to understand, Vincent, okay?"

Standing waist-deep in a dead ocean, I see. In my hands, Amelie's suicide note: a pulpy, soggy mess.

The rolling of waves becomes the wailing of a child. High-pitched and cutting.

"Open your eyes, Vincent. You have to see now."

I see. It is not the remnants of a letter in my hands. It is my shriveled heart. Blood slick and glistening greasily in a blindingly burning sun. The baby screaming itself breathless.

The baby who was aborted because I couldn't be a father to it. Wouldn't. Didn't want to.

"Please, just open your eyes and see."

I open my eyes. I'm standing at the edge of the rocky cliff now, drowned in the shadow of a lighthouse.

Not Amelie.

It's me.

"Do you see, Vincent?"

Amelie is gone.

I am rocking on the cliff edge, screaming out her name until my voice breaks like porcelain.

Amelie isn't here.

She was never here.

There was never a lighthouse. There were no cliffs.

"Can you understand, Vincent? Amelie is still alive. She never died. You tell yourself that she killed herself because you couldn't cope. With your illness, with losing your job, the abortion, and then with the end of the relationship. With her discarding you after you'd lost everything. But she's very much alive. She's happy. Healthy. Look, Vincent. You need to look at the picture now."

Staring transfixed into an ocean dark, stark, infinite.

It's raining. My clothes are soaked through.

Raindrops trickle, dripping into my eyes. Burning. I am full of rainwater.

"Look, Vincent. She's alive. She's happy. You know this. She moved back to the States. She has a child now. She got back together with her husband, and they have a baby girl. A family. We've been trying to introduce you to all of this slowly, delicately. But that method hasn't been helping your recovery. We need you to accept this now and work with us. Work with us, Vincent."

I open my eyes.

The sun is a blinding white.

The computer screen is a blinding white.

Colors take form. Shapes drift, shift, converge.

Katherine's breath on my face. Her words coffee-drenched. "What do you see, Vincent?" she asks, clicking at the computer mouse, causing another picture to slide into view.

My eyes sting. I twist my neck, flinching away from Katherine's voice and the illuminated screen.

I'm in Katherine's office.

My mother and father are sitting together on the small, two-person sofa next to the bird of paradise plant. Their eyes glisten in the lamplight, full of rainwater. My mother's biting her bottom lip and watching me. She looks desperate. Desperately sad. Desperately hopeful.

I don't know why. My head hurts so much.

"Look at these pictures and tell me what you see, Vincent."

I turn to Katherine. I stutter into a fist pressed to my mouth, stammering, "I see her... I see Amelie... She's alive... Not dead... Happy with her family. Her husband. And her child. Her baby daughter." I spit the words out like broken teeth.

"We need you to say the truth for you to get better, dear," my mother says, squeezing my father's hand.

In my own hands, Amelie's letter. The suicide note she left behind. I slowly unfold it, knowing already what's on it.

Nothing.

The paper is blank. Just a blank piece of lined paper that has been folded and unfolded a thousand times over. It's falling to pieces like snowflakes in my palms.

"Vincent, do you accept that you're not allowed to see or contact her again?"

"Yes." I nod slowly. "The restraining order. I remember now. I know."

"You can't get better and get out of here if you don't accept what went wrong, Vincent," my mother murmurs. Squeezing my father's hands so tightly, the blood drains from both of their fingers.

I close my eyes. Force myself to see the things I painted black within my mind.

I was eight the first time I tried to hang myself.

When I was 28, I did it again.

The last fight with Amelie. She shoved the ultrasound scan of the baby in my face for the last time. I couldn't take it anymore. I pried it from her fingers, and I tore it to pieces. Scattering it over us both like snowfall. The noise that flew from her lips, I'll never forget. It was an animal sound of absolute breathless agony. She stumbled and fell from my apartment, grasping at her stomach. I watched her slowly make her way down the hallway, clinging to the walls for support. Before I closed the door on her, she turned to whisper, "I fucking hate you more than you'll ever know, Vincent."

I didn't blame her. I hated myself. I was a piece of shit. Spreading my mental illness to those I loved like a sexually transmitted disease. Chlamydia mind. Syphilitic heart. A man born to hang.

I waited hours and then days for her to come back, sat on the floor amongst piles of cans and bottles. She never did. Come back.

I didn't know it then, but that would be the last time I would ever hear her say my name. She had never forgiven me for the abortion. Sometimes, I think she only stayed around to inflict as much trauma on me as I had on her. I didn't fight it. I didn't blame her. I was a piece of shit, after all.

I tried calling her. Didn't know what I wanted to say. I wanted to hear her voice. Her number was dead. I just got the same robotic message on repeat down the line. "The number you have dialed is temporarily unavailable, please try again later. The number you have dialed is temporarily unavailable, please try again later. The number you have dialed is temporarily unavailable, please try again later."

She blocked me. When I tried from a payphone, I realized she'd changed her number. Deleted her social media. I had no way of contacting her. I drank and I waited. I didn't know what else to do.

When the phone finally rang, it was my boss's voice booming down the line. The disappointment I felt in hearing someone else's voice was crushing. He told me I was fired, and I screamed at him to go fuck himself and I hung up.

I waited for her. Sure she'd come back just like she always did.

28 days passed.

Nothing. No phone calls. No letters. No screaming outside my apartment. The silence was a death of its own.

I waited because I didn't know what else to do. I couldn't imagine life without Amelie. The idea that it was really over never entered my mind. She always came back to me. Always. We were each other's poison and each other's antidote.

Another week. Each day passing was a sickness.

When all the bottles at home were empty, I stumbled around town, spilling my guts to anyone who would listen. Went to The World's End. Got myself good and drunk. Slouching on a barstool, waiting on a *deus ex machina* that would never come. Waiting until the barman apprehensively and politely asked me to leave because I'd ignored the wiping of the tables and stark-eyed glances from the staff. Tossed my glass, smashing it onto the floor. The sounds of breaking glass made me think of everything Amelie had put me through. Everything I had put her through.

I staggered out onto the street. It was raining hard. I vomited down a drain. Hailed a taxi to the apartment Amelie shared with that stuck-up bitch, Hanna. I threw up into my lap, and the taxi driver forced me out of the cab. I tossed what cash I had into the puddle of stomach acid on the backseat and told him to go to Hell. Walked the rest of the way. The rain came down harder, and I was happy for that because it seemed fitting. Romantic. Fucking Hollywood-esque. Her bedroom lights were on. Bright yellow at 4:44 in the morning. I wondered what she was doing up so late on a work night. I held up my palms to the sky, collecting the warm rainfall in my hands like ocean water.

I can feel each individual raindrop still.

Rain burning my eyes. Standing on her street again. Full of rainwater and trembling. Sweating. Drenched in a wet fear. Burning in a fever of love, misery, confusion, regret, and illness.

The door, heavy wood. Painted a shade of dark blue.

The door has a brass knocker shaped like an urn. Ashes to ashes. Dust to dust. It's smooth and worn in places. Weathered by time and touch. I watch a hand hesitating, twitching like a drowning spider, above the knocker for a long time before the dripping fingertips fumble at the knocker and finally use it.

I bash the brass knocker back and forth many times before she finally answers.

She's in a gray T-shirt hanging down to her thighs. This should be a sign, but I am too blind. All I can see is her face. Her eyes and her lips.

The orange glow of a streetlamp is like fire set ablaze on her skin. Her hair wild. She's still wearing make-up. Smudged and smeared in places that make my stomach roll like a crocodile with something desperate between its jaws.

"Fuck! You? Please, just go home." She hisses it out on the end of a sigh, as though I'm nothing but an inconvenience.

"Amelie, you haven't been taking my calls. You've been ignoring me!"

"What the fuck do you think?" She glances behind her into the darkened hallway, closes the door a little more. "The reason I didn't answer your calls is because I didn't want to see or hear from you anymore."

"You're just going to try and ghost me after three fucking years and everything we've been through together?" Lightheaded, I place my hand against the bricks of her building for balance.

She leans further away from me. Cringing. "It's just easier that way."

"Easier? For who?"

"Look, it's really late. Just go home, okay? You're really drunk."

"I just want to talk, Amelie."

"What's the point in going over all that shit, again? It will only hurt us both, so there's really no point in talking about all that negative shit ever again."

"Look, my clothes are soaking wet. Can I just come in for a moment? Talk in your room for a little while?" My words rise and fall. I'm shaking so badly, it's a seizure. I don't know why. I don't feel cold at all.

"No, you can't." She glances back again. Readjusts the fabric of her baggy T-shirt.

"Why?"

"Because I don't fucking want you to. It's raining really hard. You turn up at my home at four o'clock in the morning, drunk out of your mind. Covered in vomit."

"It's Hollywood-esque, isn't it?"

"No, it fucking isn't. It's creepy. Like you're stalking me or something."

"Stalking? What the fuck are you talking about? Why would you even say that?"

"I'm sorry but it's true. Look, I'm really tired. I want to go to sleep. Please just go home."

"I just want to be with you again. I want to say I'm sorry for what I did."

"For what you did?"

"For losing you. For what I made you do. I want you to forgive me."

Her face tightens into sharp edges and points. "The *abortion*, you mean?" She emphasizes the word, and it's the first time I glimpse any kind of emotion in her eyes.

"Yes. For everything. I made a lot of mistakes, but I want to fix it now, I can fix it now."

"No, you can't. It's too late."

"Why won't you forgive me?" I slur, shouting. Underneath the falling rain, I feel my face flush. A car alarm starts madly honking somewhere. Lights flash on, illuminating windows down the street.

"I don't love you anymore. There's nothing left to forgive. It's over."

"Why? Can you just tell me why?"

She steps back. Slams the door in my face. The urn-shaped knocker rattles. Smirking at me. Giggling. "Go home or I'm calling the cops," she shouts through the heavy wood.

"Don't close the door on me, Amelie. Let me say goodbye to your face this last time, at least. Let me see your face one last time to say goodbye."

I hear muffled voices through the wood. A harsh conversation in the hallway. There is a long pause and then she says slowly, "I said I don't fucking love you anymore. It's really over this time. I mean it. Go. Home."

"I can't accept that. I know you love me. I can't live without you." I rattle on the door. Shaking it.

"Then pretend I'm dead because you're dead to me. My love is dead for you. I'm dead to you and you're dead to me. Everything's dead like the baby. Go back home and drink some coffee or something. Whatever, I don't fucking care."

"I love you! I want you to be my wife!" I shout through the soaked front door.

"Fuck you!" she screams back. She's crying now, and I'll never know what those last tears mean.

Rain falling from the pitch-black sky, torrential downpour, raindrops falling so slowly, they're diamond-shaped flakes of ice that shatter on my fingertips and catch the light on the wet concrete like supernovas.

The front door dripping wet underneath my fingertips.

All I have is handfuls of rainwater.

"What happened after that, Vincent? What happened next?" Katherine prompts.

She told me through the cold blankness to go away. I told her that I loved her. Told her I wanted to marry her again. It was the final card I had left to play. Maybe she loved me or maybe she didn't. To this day, I still don't know if what we had was love or a chronic illness that we'd shared for three years. A fever. A fugue state. Still don't know what was real and what wasn't.

When I put my head to the door, I thought I heard a man's voice mumbling with Amelie's. The rain hits the concrete and I finally understand the punchline to a joke I'd been told a month before. She'd always said it was easier to move on if you moved onto someone new. A replacement. I wondered if it was one of the two I knew about. Michael and Greg. I lost my temper. I called her a fucking cunt through the letter box. She shouted back that she was calling the cops.

I carved **FUCK YOU** into her front door with my own door key. There was a car parked outside her house. A shitty, souped-up Fiat. I threw a brick through the windshield, convinced it belonged to whoever was in there with her.

A neighbor opened his window to tell me to go home and sleep it off. I told him to mind his own fucking business. Maybe I threatened him. I can't remember. I don't know if it was him, Hanna, the guy, or Amelie who called the police.

I sat down on the curb outside her house, vomited and wept. That kind of funeral weeping.

When the soaked pavement, wet bricks, and her front door were illuminated by the cold blue of the police car's lights, I ran. They didn't pursue me. I took the back streets home.

An hour later, stumbling down a street near my apartment, I tried to pick a fight with a couple of kids passing a joint between themselves on a bus stop bench. They laughed and walked away. I wished I had friends. I was alone. Unconnected to everyone and everything. A fetus torn away from the umbilical cord. Discarded. A ghost. I staggered the rest of the way home, cursing the dead morning air as though it were a priest listening compassionately, nodding, and telling me that Jesus loves me and would protect me. I knew love was as meaningless as the dissipating memories of all the lips I'd ever heard it murmured from.

Almost daylight. The deep blue of being in between all things.

At home, I vomited twice more into the toilet. I knew what needed to be done. The only thing left to do.

I took a cord. Made of cotton. From a pair of gray Champion jogging bottoms Amelie used to wear as pajama pants around the apartment.

I wrapped it around my throat. The fingers on my hands worked fluently. Not impulsively, but almost instinctively.

I pulled the cord taut. Knotting and throwing the end of it over the bathroom door. Shut the door up tight.

I dialed her number on my mobile phone, erratic, screaming at the unanswered calls.

The number you have dialed is temporarily unavailable, please try again later. The number you have dialed is temporarily unavailable, please try again later. The number you have dialed is temporarily unavailable, please try again later.

Leaned forward. Dangled there, weak at the knees. Phone useless, hung limply in my hand. On my knees like a child eight years old. Red in face, bashful, ashamed. Leaned forward, wept from the pain and pitiful, fated demise.

A fade out to gray and red. Cut to black.

The phone rang out into the vacant atmosphere of everything.

"Do you want to get better, Vincent?" Katherine's hand on my shoulder. She hands me a tissue from the box on her desk, and I realize I'm crying.

"Yes, yes, I want to get better now. I want to," I choke out the words and believe them.

"You need to forgive Amelie now. Most of all, you need to forgive yourself."

TWENTY

That night after the intervention.

I awake to a red light crashing against the walls of my room. I rub at my eyes. Glance at the wristwatch Amelie gave me for our anniversary years ago. **4:45**. The brutal lights assaulting my face. I throw off the covers and blink my way through the crimson strobe and early morning gray to the window. An ambulance is parked by the entrance. The siren off. It's a repeat of something that happened a couple months ago or a couple years ago. A recovering alcoholic, bipolar man named Jim smuggled a shard of glass back into the clinic after one of the monitored outings to the local park. Slashed his wrists. Killed himself. He thought he couldn't get better. Thought it was his only escape. And he took it.

I stand there, staring through the window at the ambulance parked jaggedly in front of the main entrance, full of a deep dread like a house fire burning through my body.

I already know.

The murmuring voices and squeaking gurney wheels slowly roll down the corridor. I don't need to open my door to know it will be Beatrice's body underneath the white sheet. The paramedics take their time now that there's no need to rush. I think about her face the last afternoon I saw her. Her eyes. The deep hurt there.

In the haze, the ambulance siren lights up memories of her in a fog of blood red. I gaze around my sparse room. I look at the chair. The bed. The desk. Trying to find meaning. Reality. All the furniture seems completely alien to me now. The letters from Beatrice still crumpled, unread on the carpet by the door.

I try to light a cigarette to stop my hands from shaking. Takes a few attempts to finally get it to ignite. My whole body is ripped by tremors that sink into the marrow of my bones.

Beatrice.

I could have saved her. If I had read her letters. If I had gone to her. Told her that I loved her. That I did want her. If I told her I was sorry. I had been so mired in my own pain that I completely ignored hers.

I could have saved her life, but I didn't.

I watch them load her lifeless body into the back of the ambulance. One of the paramedics shouts something to the driver. The lights are switched off.

The ambulance leaves.

Almost daylight. The deep blue of being in between all things and nowhere.

I sit up smoking until two packs of cigarettes are empty and the morning sun creeps through the window like death itself come to sit beside me.

I leave my room and go straight down the corridor towards Beatrice's. Her room is derelict. Bare. The bed stripped to the frame. Her photographs taken from the walls. Only pinholes like bullet holes remain. Nothing. It's almost as though she was never here.

She's gone.

Later, I'm looking at the painting of the cherry blossom tree Beatrice painted. Her happy place. Someone, maybe Davina, hung it from a small plastic hook in the cafeteria. Mark shuffles next to me sideways, tells me out of the side of his mouth that he heard Beatrice used a broken Roy Orbison CD to cut her throat in the woman's lavatory. He tells me that she severed her jugular vein, and it would have been quick. Says he never did like Roy Orbison. He holds up a handful of Kleenex to me, and I only realize I'm crying again when I touch my face. It feels like rainwater underneath my fingertips.

Without Beatrice, everything feels emptier than it did before. The daylight is duller. The clinic is much colder. I stare at the painting of the cherry tree and think about Beatrice.

I swallow the pills they offer me and quickly shuffle to the bathroom to make myself vomit.

Go back to my room, so I can "meditate." So, I can be with Beatrice again. I need to go back. Stop her from killing herself. I can save her.

I read the notes she left for me.

Beatrice and I will always be shadows slow dancing in derelict rooms.

The end is never really the end.

Thanks for reading! Find more transgressive fiction (poems, novels, anthologies) at: Outcast-Press.com

Twitter & Instagram: @OutcastPress

Facebook.com/OutcastPress1

GoFund.Me/074605e9 (Outcast-Press: Short Story Collection)

Amazon, Kindle, Target, Barnes & Nobel

Email proof of your review to OutcastPressSubmissions@gmail.com & we'll mail you a free bookmark!

20 dark short stories by debut and veteran subversive writers like Craig Clevenger, Greg Levin, Lauren Sapala, Paige Johnson, Stephen J. Golds, and more! Everything from serial killers and speculative cannibals to strippers and smack addicts.

MORE FROM

OUTCAST PRESS

60+ illustrated poems told under the buzz of a bar's strip lights. Whirlwind dates devoured by sewer rats. Grief that turns into vindictive triumph. Fights that leave bartenders & bystanders picking up the bloody shards. Addictions to parties & people that claw at your complexion & mental stability. Wallowing in wine & rumpled sheets, dirty flings & dead seasons. "B F Jones' terse style pounds the reader like a red-wine-headache" ~ HLR, author of *History of Present Complaint*

MORE FROM

STEPHEN J. GOLDS

Paper lanterns & petty crime. Whiskey bars & beach confessions. One-night stands & childhoods that led to cheating, self-harm & paranoia. From OCD & grief to benign inspirations like antiseptic cream & call-waiting, Stephen J. Golds examines life with a sigh only sometimes wistful. Before an urban Japanese backdrop, we ride w/ him amid subway delays & panic attacks, careening cars & horror movies.

ABOUT THE AUTHOR

Stephen J. Golds was born in North London but has lived most of his life in Japan. As editor of *Punk Noir Magazine*, he specializes in noir writing like his crime story collection *Gone*, though is heavily influenced by transgressive fiction and dirty realism. His three fiction books can be read as a trilogy or stand-alone noir novels that deal in themes of mental trauma, betrayal, and twisted love. Such includes *Say Goodbye When I'm Gone*, *I'll Pray When I'm Dying*, and *Always the Dead*.

Golds also writes poetry with the collections *Love Like Bleeding Out With an Empty Gun in Your Hand*, *Poems for Ghosts in Empty Tenement Windows I Thought I Saw Once*, as well as *Half-Empty Doorways and Other Injuries*.

StephenJgolds.WordPress.com

Twitter: @SteveGone58

www.ingramcontent.com/pod-product-compliance
Lightning Source LLC
Chambersburg PA
CBHW030755200726
48288CB00004B/1181